COMPLEXITY
A KINKY CONNECT CHRONICLES NOVELLA

HARPER MILLER

ISBN-13: 978-0-9975447-1-8

Disclaimer

This is a novella. Not a short story, novelette, or novel. This tale features an M/M pairing. If gay erotica/erotic romance is not your cup of tea and you are offended by same-sex relationships or crass language, you should bypass this story. Content is intended for a mature audience, 18+.

Complexity is the fourth installment in The Kinky Connect Chronicles. The Kinky Connect Chronicles are short erotic stories/novelettes all wrapped up in neat little bows. These stories are standalones. No cliffhangers in the lot!

Acknowledgments

Many thanks to my beta readers—Julia, Patrice, and Kelvin—for providing valuable feedback. The soul-crushing brutality only helps me to become a better writer. xoxo ;-)
Also, thanks to my "translator" Ivan M. for assisting me with Manny's lingo.
Special thanks to Brad Vance and Jules Dixon, for listening to me bitch and ask tons of questions during various stages of writing this tale. You'll never know how much I appreciate you both taking the time out of your writing schedules to field my inane and not-so-inane questions about writing gay romance.
Stepping into another genre is a scary yet exciting process, but I was lucky to have a variety of gay romance authors share their insight on a multitude of topics.
Getting to know authors who dominate this genre has been my saving grace. Who says indie authors don't help one another out?

DEDICATION

For all the single people searching for the spark that sets your soul on fire. The game of love can be cruel, but when you find the right connection, there's nothing quite like it.

"We love because it's the only true adventure."
—Nikki Giovanni

CONTENTS

When It Hurts So Bad

Ever feel like your life isn't your own?

Deep down you know it's real, but you still can't help thinking that, at any moment, someone's going to come and shake you awake and tell you it was all a dream. Some days I expect an all-knowing voice to yell, "Aye yo, Manny, psych!"

But this ain't a dream. This is real life. My life.

Lately, this thing called Life has been torturing me, and I'm having a hard time dealing. It's like I've been sticking my hand into fire and hoping, by some miracle, I don't get burned. Any person with an ounce of common sense knows you can only play with fire for so long before it devours you.

That's what fire does, right? Consumes. Steamrolls. Destroys whatever's in its path. It ain't rocket science; it's logic. But what the hell do I know about logic?

I abandoned logic a long-ass time ago. Eventually, my luck runs out and shit reaches epic proportions. Then it only takes the smallest spark to blow the powder keg that is my life and all hell breaks loose.

Thinking like this only makes my shitty day even shittier. *Don't be a bicho quejón, Manny.* Cursing under my breath, I turn the key to open my apartment door. Before dropping my gym bag, jacket, and keys, I reach for the light switch, and then kick the door closed a little too hard. I wince. I'll probably hear about that from Mrs. Lopez later. Seems like she's constantly on my ass about the noise in and around this building. If it's not "Manny, you walk too loud," it's "Manny, your TV's too loud," "Manny, your stereo's too loud," "Manny, your dog barks too much." I don't even have a dog. Whateva. I make sure to secure the dead bolts and put the chain on the door. Better to be safe than sorry. There's been more robberies than normal lately, but Mrs. Lopez scares me more than the *cacos* on the block.

On any given night this shithole building smells like the UN's used jockstrap, but the aroma lingering in my entryway ain't the *asopao* from downstairs mixing with samosas and curry from a couple of doors away. It's me— I'm a lil' overripe.

Logic says I should grab a shower, but I head over to the minibar I've set up in the corner of my living room instead, and grab the bottle of Wild Turkey. Big pimpin' up in NYC.

I have goals. And paying mad money in rent won't get me there. Actually, it's stupid to inflate some rich dude's already fat pockets for an apartment the size of a walk-in closet. But us New Yorkers, we do it. We cram into the shittiest places in the most suspect of neighborhoods just to say we have a place "in the city." In truth, it's thirty minutes from midtown in one of the other boroughs. God forbid you live in Staten Island—fuckin' no-man's-land. You might as well consider yourself in exile.

I should've known better than to look for a no-fee apartment on Craigslist. I ain't rollin' in dough. *Yo podría quejarme.* Shit, I'm always complainin' when it comes to

2

where I live, but I'm comfortable. Setting up a minibar in the corner of this "amazing location with brand-new amenities, a recently upgraded lobby, plentiful shopping, and a nearby Starbucks" and installing a new showerhead is about as sophisticated as I'm gonna get. The only true thing about that ad was the Starbucks. I guess the management company considered "nearby" ten blocks away. Whateva. I got duped. Can't say I've got plans for any other upgrades. I'm saving up.

The liquid sloshes around in the bottle when I snatch it from its shelf, my nerves on edge and my mind racing. This shit had better make me forget . . . for a little while, at least. The crystal Old Fashioned glasses my moms gave me sparkle in the light of the streetlamp that streams through my grimy window, inviting me to be gentlemanly and proper, but I can't bother with glasses and ice cubes right now. Tonight I'm having my whiskey neat and straight outta the bottle. The copper liquid burns when it hits the back of my throat, but it's raw and soothing and just what I need.

I grab the remote off the coffee table and power up the iPhone docking station. The beat drops, and then Jay Z spits the opening lyrics of "Empire State of Mind." Not today, Jigga Man, not today.

"Skip," I mumble with my lips pressed against the mouth of the bottle and my thumb on the fast-forward button. Brittany Howard's voice rasps through my apartment as The Alabama Shakes' "Gimme All Your Love" wails from the speakers that flank the bar.

He introduced me to this band. Fucker.

The liquor smolders as I hold it in my mouth and sink onto the couch. My head falls back and I swallow, letting the melancholy lyrics and angry electric guitar riffs amplify my foul mindset. This song is taking me somewhere I didn't want to go. Now I'm stuck and in a funky-ass mood.

The kind of mood where I don't give a damn about anything or anyone. The kind of mood where the only thing I wanna do is drown my sorrows in a shit-ton of alcohol until I'm so sloppy I forget my own name. Oblivion is exactly where I wanna be.

At least I admit I drink too much. Over these last few nights me and this bottle have become besties. Ain't that some shit?

Might as well get smashed, then maybe I'll be able to get a decent night's sleep. I haven't slept right in about a week. That's a lie. I haven't slept well for about six months. Six months of tossing and turning. Six months of being one moody motherfucker. Six months of being chill one minute, then pissed off the next.

My friends think I'm fuckin' nuts. My own brother won't come anywhere near me. I can tell he wants to have a heart-to-heart, but I don't have it in me to tell him why I'm a basket case. To me, he's still a kid, even though he's grown, has a good job, and a girlfriend he's been shackin' up with—but I don't want him to look at me differently. It's stupid, and I'm probably overreacting, but Juan and I have a good relationship. I can't jinx it. We're all we've got: me, Moms, and the kid. We're one tight-knit family, and I wanna keep it that way.

I've got emotional ADD, and the shit's so bad my stomach's twisted. But I don't feel anything 'cept empty.

After toeing off my kicks, I try to find a comfortable position. This right here is good: Me with a death grip on a bottle of booze, ass planted on the couch, and feet propped up on the coffee table. When I finally settle, taking a couple of deep breaths to ease the tension in my body, my phone vibrates.

I sit up and place the bottle on the table before digging the phone outta my pocket. I glance down at the screen and frown the moment I recognize the name.

Of course it's him. *Fuck him.*

I ignore the call and turn on the ringer—forgot to do that after my last client. Can't afford to miss any calls when you're self-employed, but you sure as shit can screen 'em. The couch cushions are tryna swallow me whole, and I'm not putting up much of a fight. I'm beat. My body is worn down, and I know I look like shit because I feel like shit. I wanna muster up enough energy to shower and sleep, but I know sleep won't come.

Look at me, winning all over the fuckin' place.

Why does everything have to be so complicated?

My voicemail alert chimes, but I delete the message without so much as a listen, and then toss the phone across the couch. *Just leave me alone.* I haven't seen him in a week and haven't answered any of his calls, either. Was that a punk move? Yeah, but it's what needed to happen. I ghosted because I thought we needed some space. For once I was being smart. Giving us both time, ya know, to figure out what the fuck we're doing. I have no clue where this thing is going. Even worse, I don't know what the hell this *thing* is. And I doubt he has any idea how I feel about him . . . or maybe he does.

Never in my life have I been so confused. Am I still bi if I only wanna be with a dude? Well, one dude, specifically? My sexuality has never been an issue, but now I got questions and feelings and fuckin' feelings about feelings, man.

Here I am, trying to put myself into a box, and it pisses me off. Why does it have to be either-or? Why do I need to put a label on who I am? I know how I feel. I still enjoy women, but when I'm with him, I . . . I don't want anyone else. No other women, no other men. Just him.

I *crave* him. Seeing him with Armand shouldn't have rattled me, but it did.

It was a just another Wednesday on set. Those early starts made waking up a bitch. Filming wasn't scheduled to begin until nine, but I wasn't there for that anyway. I was hired to put the film's star through hell. The good thing about a six a.m. private training session is that I could get my daily workout in and get paid for it. I beat my own ass that day in a grueling shoulder, chest, and ab workout, and still had time for a decent shower before I headed back to my studio and my other clients. I took my time getting changed, luxuriating in a trailer that was doper than most of the hotels I'd been in. My mini-vacation was over, so I headed to grab something from Craft Services before I made my way across town when I saw *him* hanging out with the crew laughing and shooting the shit. No biggie. He was a friendly guy, but what bothered me was the full-on flirt session he was having with the costume designer.

I shouldn't have felt threatened, but I was. I had no right to be. We weren't an item, but this old queen had me feeling territorial. Everybody on set knew Armand. Even though he had about twenty years on me, he was a head-turner even without his flamboyance. Armand wrapped his willowy body in a pair of pinstriped black pants and a light gray button-down that had like three buttons undone, exposing a whorl of chest hair. Despite being old as fuck, he was still a good-lookin' dude. He looked like a shape-shifting cartoon villain with his tightly coiffed hair streaked with silver, soul-stealing hazel eyes, and a nose so sharp he put me in mind of a bird of prey. I half expected Armand to take flight in the middle of all his overexaggerated hand-talking.

A frown formed on my face as I watched Armand sidle up and paw all over *him* and even go so far as to brush wet hair from *his* face. I wanted to slug the guy for touching what was mine, but that's the thing: He wasn't mine. I had no say in who flirted with him. I had no say in who touched him. I wanted to think it didn't mean anything, since Armand had a hard-on for anything attractive with a cock, but seeing *him* get groped like that, even playfully, made me wanna deliver a beatdown. Weren't there sexual harassment laws in place to prevent that type of shit? No part of costume designing was involved in what was happening.

I was almost willing to overlook it and quit being paranoid. But when our gazes met, it was like he was tryna make me jealous with this Armand shit. There were tons of people around—there's always somebody lurking who makes it their business to be in everybody's business—so it wasn't like I was about to flirt and say some inappropriate shit around all those nosy motherfuckers. I knew better than to fraternize like that in public, but I wondered if he was testing me to see how I would react. Why bother tryna make me jealous? We were nothing to each other but distractions. Sexual distractions.

Right. This . . . whatever it is . . . ain't nothin' but a sexual distraction. Maybe if I say that shit enough, I might actually believe it.

So much has changed in six months. We've grown closer, more—I don't know—intimate? Does that even make sense? And now . . . now, my feelings are coming to a head. Heh, head. What I wouldn't give right now to feel his lips wrapped around my dick. I miss his mouth milking me dry, like my seed was some sort of prize and he was desperate to win top honors.

We both fooled ourselves into believing we could have sex and nothin' but bomb-ass orgasms would come from it. "Fuck buddies" sounds like a cool arrangement, right? Wrong.

What makes this not just a friends-with-benefits deal is that neither of us ever addressed the 800-pound gorilla in the room: exclusivity. We never talked about it, never brought it up. Whenever one of us headed in that direction, the other found a detour.

He didn't know it then, and probably doesn't know it now, but I haven't hooked up with anyone else since we started fucking. I mean, he might have figured that out. When I wasn't working or spending time with friends and family, I was with him. There wasn't time for me to fool around with other people even if I wanted to. But the thing is, I didn't want to. I wanted to spend whatever free time I had with him. He never asked me outright if I was seeing anyone else, but I think he'd wanna know if I was, right? Well, my guess is he would wanna know. I dunno.

Merengue blares from my phone, startling me outta my thoughts, thank God. I love that damn ringtone. Elvis Crespo's "Suavemente" reminds me of Mom Dukes making *pasteles* and cleaning our apartment every Saturday morning, and my brother, thinkin' he was slick, sneaking into our room and nudging me awake just to beg me to make him breakfast and watch some cheesy-ass show with him. Why he couldn't've asked Moms to make him something or even fix the shit himself was beyond me. Cereal was easy enough. But that's the price I paid as a big brother. And those TV shows, yo—I suffered through entirely too many episodes of *Power Rangers*. What twenty-year-old watches *Power Rangers*? It was bad enough that I was legally an adult and still sharing a room with the twerp. Yeah, that threw a wrench into my sex life. The only time I could sneak anyone over was when Moms was at work and Juan was at mi titi's place. Don't even get me started on how much that arrangement fucked up my masturbation time. Beating off was kept strictly to the shower. Sharing a room with Juan was some sad shit, but we made do.

Back then, I was taking classes at Bronx Community College a few days a week, so I was always gettin' my study on, but weekends? What I lived for back in the day was sleepin' in, chillin' at Van Cortlandt Park with my boys, baggin' girls, and playin' handball.

That ringtone has healing powers like Moms' *sopa de salchichón*. Even though I'm in a shitty mood, I smile. Nostalgia like a mug. I lean across the couch to look at the display. Big surprise, it's him, *again*. The smile I had a few seconds ago quickly turns into a scowl.

I let the phone ring, and less than a minute later, the voicemail alert chimes. Curiosity is about to kill me, so I punch in my password and put the phone to my ear.

"Manny? Manny, goddamnit. Please pick up the phone. I know you've seen my incoming calls. Are you even listening to these messages? It's been a week. A week. I need to see you. We need to talk."

"If you're pissed off at me, tell me, talk to me, but don't shut down on me. I'm tired of leaving voicemails. If you want to end this and this is your way of doing it, fine. Fine! Fuck, I hate feeling like this. I'll come and see you if I have to. If you don't call me back, I'm coming uptown, Manny. We need to hash this out and talk like adults. If you're going to do this, you need to tell me it's done to my face. God, why do you do this to me, Manny? Emmanuel?"

The line goes dead and I delete the voicemail before releasing one long-ass sigh. He'll come see me? He shouldn't be anywhere near the Bronx. A pretty white boy like him has no business in my 'hood, especially a well-known pretty white boy. *Pendejo.* I don't have time for whatever game he's playin'.

I lazily scroll through my call log and press his number. It took me hitting it twice for the call to connect. The whiskey is finally kickin' in and I'm a little lit. The phone barely rings before he picks up.

"Hey," he says. The hoarse sound of his voice catches me off guard and a stabbing sensation seizes my chest. I know it's all in my head, but it's like rapid, tiny needle pricks all over my skin.

I'm a mess.

Has it only been a week since I've heard his voice? Hearing him now—just that one syllable—is painful relief. No matter what's going through my head, right now I've gotta keep my shit together.

"Hey, yourself."

"It's good to hear your voice, Manny. You've been avoiding me." Wasn't a question, but a statement—a true statement.

"Yep," I nonchalantly reply. "If you're leaving messages and callin' me 'Emmanuel,' then you must really wanna get my attention."

He lets out a half chuckle. "I've been trying to get your attention all week. I've missed your company. Care to tell me why you're shunning me?"

I avoid answering his question and ask one of my own instead. "Were you really gonna make a trip up here?"

Ever since this little thing between us started, I've always headed downtown to his place. He's never come up here. Too many things could go wrong and make a bad situation epically worse. There are mild fuckups and things you can't come back from. Me taking the trip downtown is a better bet.

"If you didn't pick up your phone, yes. I've been calling and calling and calling. And would have pounded on your door all night. I'd do whatever needed to be done until you talked to me. It's been a week, Manny. Talk to me. Tell me what's going on."

Avoiding his question again, I say, "That ain't the smartest move, *loco*. You're not exactly unrecognizable. The paparazzi would be up here with the quickness. Not to mention the cops. You don't come up here making a crapload of noise and not expect the cops to get called."

"Yeah, you're right. It was a dumb idea, but I wasn't thinking. You do that to me, you know—cause me to not think straight."

"I see," I respond with a low grunt. He always does that shit. Make comments about how I affect him. I quickly wonder if he'd been leavin' me a trail of bread crumbs all this time. Hope slams against my rib cage. Does he have feelings for me too?

"Can I see you, Manny?" he asks, his voice that syrupy-sweet tone he uses when we're in bed. The shit that sucker punches me right in the gut. And now I'm hot, but for an altogether different reason.

"What do you need to see me for? Armand not occupying enough of your time?" I was being a dick, but whateva.

"Ah, so now we're getting somewhere. That's why you've been avoiding me? Because of Armand?"

I remain silent.

"Manny?"

"What?" I can't deal right now. Not with the way he says my name. . . . *Manipulative bastard.*

"Come see me. Let's talk about it."

"Nah. No need." I'm acting like a pissy bitch, but I don't care. "Got a client in the morning and have to be up early."

"Fine, you won't come here, then I'm coming to you."

"Didn't we just agree that that is a dumb idea? What the fuck are you doing?"

"You might not want to talk, Manny, but clearly some things need to be addressed. Avoiding the issue won't make it go away. We need to straighten this out, *now.*"

"*Mierda,*" I mumble under my breath.

"I'll be there in an hour," he says before hanging up, leaving me no time to talk him out of it.

I almost fling the phone across the room, but if I do, I won't have shit to use once it's broken. I bite down on my tongue to tamp back my anger, and I ain't tasting whiskey no more.

He's an idiot. An idiot for comin' into my space. An idiot for putting himself out there like that. So what if I wouldn't go to him? I had been tryna put some distance between us, but it only seemed to make shit more difficult for me, and there is only one explanation.

Love. I'm in love with a guy, and I'm so fuckin' angry. Angry because I can't do anything about it. I tried to fight it, and I mean hard, but the way I reacted to his voice and to him threatening to trek up to my apartment, risking shit just to talk to me, tells me all I need to know.

I am in love with Christopher.

Being honest with myself is difficult, but what's worse is nothing can ever develop between us, which is why I need to squash this thing now so we can go our separate ways.

This—whatever this is—has gone on too long. But the problem with time is that it leaves room for familiarity to settle in. Now I'm payin' the price and dealing with crap I haven't felt in a long while for anyone, let alone a man.

How I ended up in this fucked-up situation is a whole lotta crazy, but the God's honest truth.

It all started a year ago. . . .

THE SCORE

The life of a personal trainer has its pros and cons. Irregular hours, overtly flirtatious clients—I never mix business with pleasure—and sometimes crap-ass pay if I couldn't maintain a steady client base. Sometimes things were good, and sometimes I found myself struggling to keep my head above water to make shit happen, even after ten years. Two days a week were spent at Equinox downtown, and the remaining days I rented gym space in Gramercy Park. Livin' the dream. A dream that had me staying at home while I finished school and got my certifications, all of which I paid for myself. A dream that I did whatever it took to achieve aside from stealing, cheating, or killing.

My studio was small and all my equipment bought at auction, but nobody could tell me nothin'. Every move I made was another step toward my goal of opening a larger space and solely catering to high-end clientele. Then I'd hire one or two trainers and an administrative assistant to keep everything organized. I was on my way to becoming my own boss full-time instead of bouncing back and forth between Equinox and the studio. If I busted my ass nonstop for a few years I could probably retire by fifty-five.

At the time I had about six clients outside of Equinox. The money was good, of course, but it coulda been better. I knew rich people could be some penny-pinchin' motherfuckers, but I had some awfully generous clients.

For the past couple of months, I had been training this guy I liked to call "The Architect." Dude always got me stoked. Without fail, I would find myself in the shower after our sessions, poundin' my meat. It probably seemed pervy, but he had this hot-as-fuck preppy-nerdy thing goin' on—the complete opposite of me. I was hood but cleaned up nice. This dude? Real prim and proper-like, always in a suit and these thick-rimmed black glasses when he would arrive for our appointments. This guy screamed corporate professional, but I swear every time he came to the studio for our sessions, my dick instantly got hard. Tryna come up with creative ways to hide my erection was some stressful shit. Usually, I ended up holdin' a pair of boxing gloves in front of my dick, tryin' not to give away the tent in my shorts.

Things were never really that bad. I kept everything strictly professional, but that didn't mean I wasn't checking him out while I spotted him during sets. I was discreet, not only because he was my client and I didn't want to jeopardize my business, but because I wasn't exactly out about my tendency to fool around with guys when the mood struck. Only a handful of people knew about that part of me, and I wanted to keep it that way.

I'm bisexual. I'd been sexually active with women—many women. Shit, I'm a bona fide *Boricua* pussy magnet. But I've also been with men, although lately it had only been in a couples capacity. I'd had moments when I wanted solo action, but for the most part, I liked messin' around with couples. (Cue the "So, you're one of *those* types" comments.) Lately, I preferred to have dick with a side of pussy. Or maybe I was just being a greedy motherfucker. Whateva, yo. I was used to it. Heard it from guys too many times when I would go cruising. Doesn't matter if I was at a club or online, someone always had some smart-assed shit to say. Online it was worse, though. Seemed like it was always some know-it-all poppin' up in my message box sayin' that I was insecure or in denial and not comfortable with my true self, but you know what? They could say whatever the fuck they wanted. Those people didn't know jack shit about me.

But since we're talkin', I might as well put it all out there. Truth is, I've never wanted to date dudes exclusively. I know that makes me sound like an asshole—I'm not sayin' it couldn't or wouldn't ever happen, but before now it hadn't, and that was probably because I am an emotional retard. Fuck bein' PC, let's be real. I can barely connect with a woman, so guys would probably be just as much, if not more, of a pain in the ass. I mean . . . anything is possible, but like I said, I've never wanted to be in a relationship with a guy before. Even if I had, it wouldn't have mattered, because me and relationships are like spit on a hot stove.

I'd been a member of kinkysinglesconnect.com for about three years. During that time, I'd met a few couples on the site, and we'd had a blast. Actually, I'd had some of the best sex with people I met on the site. No shit was off-limits. From mild to wild, anything goes. I initially joined to connect with freak-nasty couples lookin' for a third. The ladies tended to list themselves as "single with a twist," somethin' I was totally down with. Boyfriends wanted some action, too. *You want me to fuck your lady, you swallow my load, and lick my nuts after I come? Say no more. I'm in.* Shit, sometimes I even plowed the guys.

I like sex. I like sex with men and women. I never needed a chick present to admit I liked cock. Sometimes I feel like gettin' down with a dude, sometimes I don't. When the mood hits me, I'm in it to win it. But guys who use women as buffers annoy the fuck outta me.

Anyway, I was horny as hell one night, so I hit up kinkysinglesconnect looking for a quick blow job. The Architect got some shit started, and I wanted nothing more than to get rid of my load by sliding my dick in between the lips of an eager little bottom. I was itching for a solo encounter. My dick felt like it had been in a vise from trying to suppress a constant hard-on all evening, so some out-of-this-world head from a clean-cut, nerdy professional-type would have been the perfect ending to my night.

Although I envisioned someone like The Architect meeting my needs that night, his type wasn't what I was usually into. Not trying to be a jerk or fat shame anybody, but I have a type. I watch bodies all day. Anyone I was interested in sexually should value the human form as well, and prioritize keeping their body in the best possible condition. There is something about the hard planes of the male body that turns me on. I dunno if it's the broad shoulders or the narrow waist and shoulder-to-hip ratio that got my ass all hot and bothered, but I enjoy the hell out of it. I'm not much into the bodybuilding types even though I look like one. I prefer someone that's kinda the opposite of me. Ripped but not over the top, you know?

Scrolling through the profile questions gave me a minute to really think hard on what I was looking for. If the guy was hung, that was cool, but nothin' too crazy. Maybe I liked a challenge, or maybe I wasn't completely selfish in bed, because a hefty cock in my hands or in my mouth was like hittin' paydirt, but I wouldn't blow just anybody. I once had an eager bottom who was packing a nine-incher. And holy shit, was he a horse-dick motherfucker. Lesson learned. I'd try not to choke myself to death the next time I felt generous.

As far as what positions worked for me, I topped. I'd do a flip-flop if I ever met someone I trusted. But since I ain't ever been in a relationship with a dude, I wasn't about to offer up my ass to some guy I hooked up with on a whim or was casually fuckin'. Shit, he'd better consider himself lucky to get my real name instead of an alias. For me to give some dude I barely knew that kind of power over me? Nah, it wasn't happening. Someone topping me was just . . . well, mad personal, to be honest.

I set up my "new and improved" profile to cater to what I was looking for this time around. Nobody'll talk to you without a profile. You couldn't even access any decent features on KSC without havin' a profile.

When I first joined, I didn't spend too much time thinking of a username. For real though, who gave a shit what I called myself? If a guy was going to judge me based on a handle, he wasn't thinking with the right head. Right then, all I wanted was to release my load down some *papi's* throat. I couldn't have cared less about bein' smooth, but I had to at least act like I cared, otherwise I'd get a bunch of hillbilly-lookin' dudes in my inbox.

My username was boring and unoriginal: TrainerBoy3A. I wasn't tryna impress nobody, and I wasn't lookin' for a date, just a hookup.

I didn't spend too much time filling out the next few portions, so I typed in the first things that came to mind.

Likes: Uncut dicks, cock rings with anal plugs attached, bottoms with hungry holes, tattoos, docking/frotting (tried this a few times with guys I've hooked up with more than once, looking to try it again), every once in a while a twink. Got a thing for Europeans. If you're Euro and uncut, hit me up. Tats aren't necessary, but I have a couple so I hope you like them.

Dislikes: Flakes, drugs (smoked weed years ago, not into that scene anymore), fisting, and piss. I can get into some fetishes, but miss me with that bodily fluids kink.

You: Be D/D free and discreet. No exceptions. You do you, and I do me. I don't care if you're closeted, but I'm not into closeted marrieds. I've had fun with couples who were looking for a third but I'm not looking for couples right now. When I'm ready, I'll update my profile, thanks. Bi top here, lookin' for a single dude w/no attachments. SINGLE. I don't need complications. If I like you, we may meet more than once. If not, enjoy the ride for what it's worth.

Sure, my profile was a little aggressive and probably had me coming off as a total asshole, but it kinda weeded out the weirdos. Although, creepy dick bandits were rarely deterred.

Last, I added my zip code and stats.

Age: 35
Weight: 202 lbs
Height: 6'0"
Race: **Hispanic/Latino**

Yeah, I said Hispanic/Latino. I hated when people did that shit where they'd say, "Well, Hispanic isn't a race but an ethnicity." This country is so caught up in checkin' off boxes and tryna categorize people. Who gives a fuck, really? Those people *and* the Census Bureau could fuck off. I was whatever I wanted to be. Why did I have to identify as any one thing? Why couldn't Hispanic be both my racial and ethnic identity?

Once that was all filled out, I uploaded a few pictures. The photo I ended up choosing for my main profile picture was a typical bathroom selfie of me in a pair of blue boxers. The other pics I included were shots of me in a pair of basketball shorts at the gym flexing in front of the mirror, and another was one of my professional shots I used strictly for cruising. All of the pictures showed off my physique but not a single one included my face. Rule number one: Never upload a face shot; always try to stay under the radar. If I felt a dude was cool enough, I'd send a face shot or hop on Skype.

I had been hungry as hell, but the urge to get my dick wet had overruled the need for food. It had finally caught up to me, though. My stomach was growlin', so I went in the kitchen to grab something to eat while I waited for the messages to come in. When I got back about fifteen minutes later, I had a few messages on my screen. I scrolled through them and started reading.

VersMasc4U: Have any cock shots?

ChelseaBadBoy: Let me see your face.

xxxTwinkie23: How big is your dick?

DrillNRight: You always top? How'd you like to try bottoming tonight? You can be my power bottom.

Jock492: Hot bod. Would definitely like to ride you.

TravEU: I see you're into docking and you like European men. German guy visiting NYC here, I've got a 10-inch uncut cock. Let's get together and create some hot foreskin magic.

That last message, really? "Hot foreskin magic"? That was some lame bullshit. Never in a million fuckin' years would I have led with those whack-ass lines. Damn, could I at least get a "What's up?" or "How are you?" I knew how things went—I wasn't some new kid on the block. I was lookin' for a nut. I didn't always invest in chitchat when cruising, but would it have been so bad to at least get some sort of convo going? When I approached couples, I never dove headfirst into the nitty-gritty of what I wanted. It only ended up makin' me look like a pushy douchebag.

My libido was waving a white flag and whispering, "Fuck it, Manny, it ain't worth it. Cut your losses while you can." Wasn't saying I needed a damn dissertation in my message box, but would an introduction be too much to ask for before a dude started sizing up my cock and suggesting I do shit with him I didn't do with just anyone? Sure, I was looking for a quickie but Jesus, could I catch a break?

It finally clicked that this was a bad idea. A bad idea that was giving me the kind of headache that started at the back of my head and slowly traveled through my skull and throbbed behind my right eye socket. If this was what I got within the first couple of minutes of updating my profile, then I shoulda thrown in the towel. This shit was exactly the kind of crap I got on Grindr and why I left there in the first place. No rapport was needed on Grindr. All that mattered was where you were located and how quickly you could meet for a fuck. Kinkysinglesconnect was kinda like that too, but it catered to people with more specific tastes. It also catered to people who were a bit higher quality. KSC was supposed to spare me from the legion of assholes. In this case, kinky professionals did not mean classy. So much for shootin' my load down some *papi's* throat. Looked like I would have to settle for the drain. Such a damn waste.

Irritated, and with an asphyxiating case of blue balls, I'd decided I'd had enough. But an incoming message pinged before I could snap my laptop shut.

Hey. Nice chest. Well, nice everything. Mind if I ask how much you bench?

First thing I noticed was his screen name: TightAss247

A shit-eating grin took over my face. Now we were talkin'. Twenty-four seven? Let's hope he was ready for a late-night check-in. I was disappointed that he didn't have a profile picture, but still, I was curious enough to click on his profile and read more about him. At least he didn't ask me about my dick. He had my attention for that alone.

Username: TightAss247

Age: 31
Weight: 198 lbs
Height: 6'2"
Race: White

Likes: Discreet meetings, working out, take-charge tops, dirty talk, jocks, bears, mutual masturbation, edging.

Dislikes: Druggies and drama. Also, not into twinks.

You: No drugs/STIs. Down to earth and cool. In my daily life, I come across more than enough self-absorbed people, so a laid-back fuck buddy would be ideal. Would like someone I can get off with regularly, but I guess we'll see. I'm partial to beefy Dominant-types in the bedroom. Daddy Doms are okay too. I'm also willing to experiment with a variety of fetishes, if I trust you. I'm open to new things, but my trust isn't automatic. If we get along and have an ongoing casual thing, maybe we can push my limits.

Okay, I was more than interested. Pretty fuckin' interested. He listed his race as white, but no mention of being European, damn. It wasn't a deal-breaker, but I knew what I liked.

Europeans. It was the accents, yo. My New York accent has been considered hot, so it was a win-win for me. Early last year I had a weeklong fling with a British banker who had been visiting the States on business. About a month before that, I saddled up a Turkish NYU grad student in the bathroom of a club.

Before I started daydreamin' and replayin' old times in my head, I needed to focus on the matter at hand: gettin' some action. Usually, I was immediately suspicious when dudes didn't have pics. Things were no different this time around, but he opened with a question about weightlifting—one of my favorite hobbies—which earned him a quick reply anyway. (Okay, keepin' it really real, I was dyin' to know if he was Euro and uncut, but I wasn't gonna be an asshole and ask right out the gate. Gotta abide by that golden rule shit and do unto others.)

TrainerBoy3A: 300 on a good day, you?

TightAss247: Lately? 250 if I'm lucky. Been slacking off, which means my numbers probably aren't as good as they used to be.

TrainerBoy3A: Cool. Well, dedication gets results. Stick with it and you'll see a change. Where you located?

TightAss247: SoHo, you?

TrainerBoy3A: Not too far from East 210th.

TightAss247: Hmm, the Bronx. 4 Train, Mosholu Parkway, right?

TrainerBoy3A: Yep. That too far for you? I did list my zip code.

TightAss247: Don't know if it's too far yet, let's see how this conversation goes first. I searched for guys with pics currently online. Didn't look at zip codes. You looking to meet tonight?

TrainerBoy3A: Ideally, yeah. I'd like something to pop off tonight.

TrainerBoy3A: **You Euro?**

TightAss247: No, plain ole American, but I'm uncut, does that win me some points? :)

TrainerBoy3A: Oh, most def.

TightAss247: Liked your pics. You have a hot body. Have any face shots?

I woulda said thanks, but seriously? Man didn't have shit to offer me in the way of a photograph, and he wanted to be greedy? Bold move. So what if he didn't ask about my dick, he was no different from those other guys. All wanting something for nothing.

I was feelin' the initial interaction but it was always something on these sites. I take a few deep breaths and try not to type back some rude bullshit. I retype my sentences a couple of times before I finally hit send.

TrainerBoy3A: You've gotta be kidding me. You don't have a single pic uploaded and you're asking me for a face shot? Come on.

TightAss247: Hehe, it was worth a try. I have to be discreet due to my job, that's why I don't have pics up. Hope that's not a problem?

This exchange shoulda ended right there. I smelled a catfish, and ain't nobody got time for that. No pics and a worn-out excuse? He couldn't even upload a body shot due to his job? A *body shot*? Fuck outta here. I wasn't buying it.

My headache went from mildly annoying to "it'll get worse before it gets better" in a matter of seconds. Why did I even bother?

TrainerBoy3A: I'll cut to the chase. I'm not tryna be here all night chattin'. I like to get to know the person a little bit before we get to setting things up, but I ain't here for an online bestie. None of that back and forth in messages for an eternity crap. I want to shoot my load down some lucky guy's throat tonight. Are you that somebody? At least I have body shots, but you're not giving me anything here. What's up with that?

TightAss247: You make a fair point.

TightAss247: I could be that guy. I guess time will tell. I can do a body shot. No nudes though, at least not yet. That cool?

TrainerBoy3A: Yep, send away.

A few seconds later, I received a picture via the instant messenger. I enlarged that sucker and let out a low whistle. Shit, his body was nice. Real nice. My eyes focused on his pecs before traveling down to the shredded six-pack abs he was showin' off. His profile said he was two inches taller than me, but he was definitely leaner. Wouldn't get any complaints from me. I was satisfied with what I saw.

The picture he sent was taken outdoors on a bright and sunny day in front of a pool and a waterfall surrounded by an assortment of exotic plants. He had a nice golden tan goin' on, and there was a slight sheen that made his skin glow. Was he oiled up or was that sweat? My balls suddenly got heavy. I noticed his nipples were erect, and my dick extended a not-so-gentle reminder of why I was looking at this guy's pic in the first place. The entire scene looked chill, but I was skeptical. Skeptical because the photo looked too perfect. It was mad pristine, even for a body shot. I swore to God I was being catfished.

TrainerBoy3A: Location doesn't look like anything I've ever seen in SoHo but nice bod . . . Whoever it is. Tell him to hit me up if he's looking to play.

TightAss247: What?

TrainerBoy3A: Look, I don't have time to dick around. You can't even send me a real pic? Why'd you even bother messaging me?

TightAss247: Whoa, whoa, whoa. Wait a sec, that is me. And the pic wasn't taken in SoHo, it was taken at a friend's home in Malibu last summer.

TrainerBoy3A: Okay, if that's really you, shouldn't be too difficult to snap a body shot now, right? No face, just your bod. Doesn't have to be nude. Let's see the goods, bro. You've seen what I got, what are you offering? Let me see if you're the real deal.

There was a long pause. When I say long, I mean loooong. At least ten minutes passed since I sent my last message. I knew he was bullshittin' me. Couldn't even get a blow job without dudes tryna catfish my ass. I was getting ready to place my cursor on the "X" and log off before calling it a night, but my instant messenger pinged again.

He sent a picture. It was your typical bathroom selfie body shot, except his underwear were low—so low I could see the outline of the top of his dick. He was sportin' a semi, and thick was an accurate description. I thought his body was hot before, but now in an unstaged shot, I saw just how perfect he really was. His build was impressive. It looked like he'd leaned out even more since the summer pic, and had less muscle definition. No doubt, I'd still fuck him.

TightAss247: That good enough for you? ;-)

I couldn't help but laugh. This motherfucker liked to please and put up when pushed. I got the feeling I might not get my dick sucked tonight, but he would be fun for something down the line. Yeah, this could be real interesting.

TrainerBoy3A: Perfect. I was sportin' a chub, but you're building me up to my full potential. What's your name?

TightAss247: Vinnie.

He typed that too quick. *Way* too quick. Vinnie my ass.

TrainerBoy3A: You're totally bullshittin' me, aren't you?

TightAss247: lol, yep. Tonight, I'm Vinnie.

TrainerBoy3A: All right, "Vinnie," we'll stick with that. You gay or bi?

TightAss247: Thought you didn't care as long as I wasn't a closeted married guy. Why does it matter what I call myself?

Damn, Vinnie, defensive much? Tone couldn't really be implied via text, but the way I read that shit, there was some venom attached.

TrainerBoy3A: Just making small talk. I don't care what you are as long as it ain't married.

TightAss247: No. Not married and not in a relationship.

TrainerBoy3A: That your choice?

TightAss247: No.

Okay, clearly I was askin' the wrong questions. Here I was, tryna to be courteous before I jumped into asking to meet up to get some head, but was met with standoffish asshole vibes. *Hot* standoffish asshole vibes, but still asshole vibes. Had to wonder if it would even be worth it at that point. I shoulda just called it a night and went to bed, but I was a sucker—a sucker for a hot body, apparently. Fuck.

You woulda thought I'd asked if his dog died. Maybe it wasn't as serious as I was making it out to be, and I was projecting, but if he was bitter about being single, then welcome to my world, bro. I'd been dating and fuckin' since I was fourteen and I still hadn't found my LEGO piece.

Everybody always went with the cliché shit about "searching for their missing puzzle piece." Nah, I was all about the LEGO. You know how much of a bitch it is to break them motherfuckers apart? LEGO pieces have staying power. They're the ride-or-die toy. Once they snap in, it takes hella effort to separate 'em. And forget about if you step on one. You're wincing in pain and cursing everything under the freakin' sun. But LEGO pieces are unique and indestructible. You can't help but wonder how such a small piece of plastic could fuck up your world yet make you happy at the same time. That's what I imagined love to be like—well, relationships in general. When you found the right one, all of the annoying crap was kind of rewarding.

So, yeah, I had my eye out for that someone who could hang for the long haul. The one who could make me laugh, who would support me through the good and the bad, who would see the real me and accept me, flaws and all. My LEGO piece must be trapped in a couch cushion or some shit.

Maybe "the piece that fits" will turn up, or not. I don't know what it is, but I never really thought much about settlin' down until I found myself closer to forty than thirty. It was sobering as hell to see *corillos* from the block settling into fatherhood. Knuckleheads I used to smoke blunts with were now responsible for tiny humans. That was a serious dose of reality.

I wasn't one of those guys who pretended they'd rather have a root canal than fall in love. There was no shame in admitting I wanted it. Who wouldn't want to wake up next to someone they couldn't get enough of? Knowing that someone cared about them as much as they cared about you. I wanted all the sappy shit that came with love—the crazy heart palpitations, the sweaty palms, the nerves, the dopey grins, the first kiss, the jittery feeling when you lay eyes the person you'd do anything for. I dug that shit, but it'd been a long while since I'd been in love, and I don't even know if what we'd shared *was* love. Maybe it was just some good pussy. Honestly, I didn't even know if it would ever happen for me. Me and relationships didn't see eye to eye. Maybe I'd been doing it wrong or something.

I couldn't say that I'd ever had a real connection with someone.

Might have something to do with the fact that I did more fuckin' than datin'. My last long-term relationship was with an attractive Haitian woman named Joulie. That fizzled out about four years ago. Things started off cool; my attraction to her was purely physical at first. She wasn't just hot, she was smart and funny too, with a small waist and tits to die for. I woulda ate a mile of her ass just to find out where the corn came from. Hittin' it from the back was my favorite position. I'd always been fond of a nice ass, no coincidence there.

Truth be told, I noticed Joulie's ass when she was leaving a yoga class at Equinox, and I couldn't stop staring. We crossed paths at the juice bar, where I sparked up a conversation. We chatted for about twenty minutes before

I asked her to grab a drink with me later that night. I didn't usually date women who worked out at my gym, but I was drawn to Joulie. She gave off this relaxed, fun, and flirty vibe. We got along well and dated seriously for about a year and a half. Sounds great, right?

You see, Joulie thought I was *the one*, but she wasn't *the one* for me. I liked her. I enjoyed spending time with her, but I couldn't see myself married to her. Worst of all? I didn't love her. Well, not in *that* way. Remember all that sappy shit I said? Never happened with her. Needless to say, things didn't end so well. There was no sense in staying in a relationship when I knew my feelings wouldn't change and I couldn't be what she wanted me to be, so I broke it off. When I did, oh man, she called me some foul shit and then threw all of my stuff I'd left at her apartment out the window. Her *sixth floor* apartment window. Nothing like seeing a posse of teenagers five deep run off with a barely worn pair of cross trainers, a brand-new pair of wingtips, some dress shirts, a couple of henleys, a few pairs of jeans, and three jackets.

Me and relationships just didn't get along. There was a better chance of me running into a unicorn riding the 4 train than me falling in love.

And, as if my dating life didn't suck enough, my mother was constantly chiding me. "Man-ny, when you gon' gimme some grandkids?" I'd heard that shit twice a week, at least.

"You're so handsome, mi amor. Those eyes. The only good thing your father gave you," she would say, pinching my cheeks like I was ten years old again. "You get those bright eyes from him. Maybe your niños will inherit them too."

Those were just two in a series of quotes from my mother that ran on constant rotation. My eyes tended to stand out. Their cognac color occasionally changed to dark brown—almost black—when I got riled up. Scary as fuck to some people, but they've gotten me tons of ass. Tons. The contrast of my light-colored eyes against my tanned, yellow-brown skin made it easy for me to get ass. Gettin' laid ain't never been a problem.

I always gave the same response every time she asked. "It ain't for lack of tryin', Ma. Gotta find my better half first. Dating in New York City ain't easy."

Moms knew I swung both ways. She and Titi Lucia were the only ones in the family who knew. It wasn't like I woke up one day and said, "Ma, I'm bi." Trust me, I wish shit had gone down that way.

When I was sixteen, she caught me and my boy Alex jerking each other off in my bedroom. I thought the coast was clear since she was workin' a later shift as a CNA and Juan was spending the night with mi titi since Moms wanted to be sure he went to bed on time. Getting him up for school in the morning could be a pain in the ass if the twerp didn't get to bed on time. Guess Moms didn't trust me to handle things that night, or she wanted to give me a break since Juan's nighttime routine had been interfering with me gettin' my homework done. I didn't mind picking up the slack, but I knew she didn't wanna put everything on me. Anyway, being that Moms was working late, I took the opportunity to invite Alex over. I'd seen the way he'd been lookin' at me when we were chillin' with the crew at the park. But Moms came home earlier than expected—talk about embarrassing. Imagine my mother's face when she saw me buck-ass naked with my friend's dick in my hand and his hand gripping my cock. Morti-fucking-fyin'. I've never had anything to hide from her, but the way I came out wasn't exactly the best.

We had a long talk after that, and luckily, Moms was cool. Let me rephrase that: She wasn't truly *cool*, she was just thankful that I liked girls, too. When all was said and done, I was a horny teenager who was all about experimenting. You never know what you like until you test the waters. Her hopes of having grandchildren weren't completely crushed. Psssh, like I couldn't have kids even if I was gay. Modern technology and adoption had made it easy, but I know Moms had everything riding on me meeting some nice girl, gettin' married, and knocking her up.

I wanted kids, but damn, could I find a partner first? And why in the hell was the burden of continuing the family legacy all on me? Moms had another kid too. I guess that's the price of being the firstborn. Mom Dukes had always been pretty easygoing when it came to me and my brother, but like any mother she had her overprotective tendencies. Shit drove me crazy, but that woman is everything to me, and I am grateful she's always had my back.

Now, Alex was another story. Jerk a dick, lose a friend. Never talked to that kid again. Sad, because he was one of the coolest dudes in my 'hood. I grew up in Morris Heights, a neighborhood that wasn't exactly petitioning for a spot to host the next GLAAD awards.

Some sections of the Bronx were a little more hardcore than others. If you were from where I was from and was into dick, you kept that shit to yourself. Alex might have been freaked that me and Moms were a bunch of *chotas*. I wasn't fuckin' stupid, and Moms definitely wasn't about to tell anyone.

If my father knew I sucked cock on occasion he'd probably flip the hell out, but what that sperm donor thought didn't matter. He hadn't mattered in a long-ass time. The asshole chose to abandon my mother, leaving her with an infant and a ten-year-old to raise alone. Last I heard, he had left NY and was living in Puerto Rico. Maybe he had a new family, but who cared? My abuela Rosa and tío Pablo kept in touch, but none of us had heard from my loser father since my brother was a baby, and we preferred it that way. Ain't no love lost there. That's some unbelievable shit, right? He acted as if we didn't exist. No birthday cards, no phone calls, no letters, and no apologies.

Trust me, we were all better off without him, but in the barrio, where my old man was from, being gay was . . . not exactly accepted. I could only imagine the shit I would get if my father and his side of the family knew about me being bi. My abuela Rosa loves me, but I honestly didn't know if she'd treat me the same if she knew. And Pablo? According to him, "*bugarróns* ain't macho."

Homophobia was the norm. You weren't a man if you were not fuckin' as much pussy as possible. Real men didn't suck dick. Real men didn't take it up the ass. Real men . . . blah, blah, blah. Up there, people didn't bat an eye when slurs and stereotypes entered a conversation. It was second nature. Was it ignorant? Oh, hell yeah. Everybody had an opinion. Even if it was complete bullshit, and it *all* was complete bullshit.

Anyway, enough about my nonexistent love life, my crazy upbringing, and why I stayed cruisin' for ass.

After a bit of silence, I realized "Vinnie" wasn't gonna say a damn thing. I shoulda logged off, but I was a dumbass. The friggin' Architect started this mess.

TrainerBoy3A: Dude, you still here? Sorry if I hit a sore spot. Wasn't my intention to get in your biz.

TightAss247: It's cool. I guess I'm just a little sensitive when it comes to being asked about my sexuality. Sorry if my curt answer came across as rude.

TrainerBoy3A: So, I guess that means you're gay, huh?

TightAss247: lol. You don't quit. Yes, I'm gay. I don't get to admit that often. If I even thought about admitting it, everything would come crashing down, and I'm not ready to take that head-on. I hide that part of me. Basically, stay silent and go through the motions.

TightAss247: Not the smartest thing but definitely the safest, at least for now.

TrainerBoy3A: Go through the motions . . . so you date chicks as decoys? We talkin' beards on standby?

TrainerBoy3A: Wait, sorry. Never mind. None of my biz. My bad. Forget I asked.

TightAss247: No, it's okay. Not like I ever really get to talk about any of this with anyone. The people in my life think that if we act like it's not true then it isn't.

TightAss247: I'm thirty-fucking-one. It's not a phase. I've always been attracted to men but didn't act on it until I was in my mid-twenties. That's a long time to sit on something you know in your heart to be the right thing for you. I can talk about it with you because you don't know my story and I don't know you. Makes it easier to admit, you know? No pressure.

TrainerBoy3A: Yeah. That's probably the best thing about the Internet, we're all anonymous behind a screen.

TightAss247: Exactly.

TrainerBoy3A: Can I ask you something?

TightAss247: Sure, go ahead.

TrainerBoy3A: You're in the spotlight, aren't you?

There was a long pause. About three minutes passed before he responded to my question.

TightAss247: What?

TrainerBoy3A: You have a high profile job or somethin'? You mentioned you didn't have pics up because of your job.

TrainerBoy3A: Hahaha, don't tell me you're my local Congressman. It's always the "family values" politicians with the whole anti-gay stance who usually end up getting caught on hookup sites lookin' for a lay. They stay cruisin' for dick, but get in front of a camera and it's all "Marriage should be between a man and a woman." Funny, marriage never enters into the discussion when they have a mouth full of cock. Slobbin' knob while wifey is clueless.

TightAss247: lol, that's funny and true. No, I'm not involved in politics.

TrainerBoy3A: I watch too much TV. When people tend to hide their sexuality like you do, that shit means they've got a lot on the line. Surrounded by people who whisper about it like it's a dirty secret. When you're high up the ranks, kinda makes it difficult to come out, or so I've heard.

TightAss247: Yeah, I guess.

Okay . . . he wasn't giving me much, but I couldn't blame him. It wasn't my business. He probably already said way more than he wanted to.

TightAss247: Anyway, what's your name?

TrainerBoy3A: Smooth way to change the subject, but no biggie. We don't have to talk about any of that. I could make up some fake name like "Vinnie," but I'll be real with you. I'm Manny.

TightAss247: lol, you're calling me out? All right, fair enough. Nice to meet you, Manny. You're cool.

TrainerBoy3A: Yeah, I am.

TightAss247: Humble too.

TrainerBoy3A: Yup.

TrainerBoy3A: I would ask you to Skype, but you're secretive. Best way to be sure my ass ain't getting the runaround is to meet up. You wanna meet for a beer tomorrow night? I already gave up on the idea of hooking up tonight. It's late, I've got a headache that's aggravating me, and I'm beat. At least with a beer we can chill in the corner of a bar or somethin'. No one pays attention to two guys grabbing a beer together.

There was another long pause. Six minutes that time. I stared at the clock debating whether or not to log off.

Who goes silent when you ask 'em out for a drink? You'd think I'd asked him to suck my dick on top of the bar while everyone watched.

I didn't have time for this paranoid bullshit.

Again, my cursor hovered over the X in the corner, and I swear to God, just as I was about to close the window, I got a message.

TightAss247: I have a counter offer. What about a drink in a private setting? No strings.

TrainerBoy3A: Depends on what you mean by private. Where?

TightAss247: The Grand Royal Hotel. It's in the financial district, not too far from the World Trade Center Memorial site.

TrainerBoy3A: That's doable. They got a decent bar?

TightAss247: I was thinking more along the lines of us having a drink in my room.

This sly motherfucker.

TrainerBoy3A: Dude, there's no need to trick me into meeting you. You wanna get me alone just say so, lol. We both came here lookin' to let off some steam.

TrainerBoy3A: Wait, your room? I thought you said you lived in SoHo?

TightAss247: lol, I do want to get you alone but it's more so we can talk in private and you know, do the beer thing. Being discreet and us meeting privately would be preferable. I promise I'll stock the minibar. If you have anything you specifically like, let me know and I'll make sure it's here.

TightAss247: I do live in SoHo, but for the purposes of our meeting, I think a hotel is better. I booked a room in case I got lucky tonight. I can extend the reservation for another night.

TrainerBoy3A: Whatever works for you, bro.

TrainerBoy3A: I'll drink whatever you have available. I'm not picky. What time were you thinking?

TightAss247: 8? Is that okay?

TrainerBoy3A: That's cool. Should be done with work by then.

TrainerBoy3A: Room number?

TightAss247: 1709

TrainerBoy3A: Cool. Anything comes up that changes the plan, send me a message via the site. We good?

TightAss247: Yeah we're good. You do the same.

TrainerBoy3A: You got it. I'll see you then.

TightAss247: Night, Manny.

TrainerBoy3A: Peace.

I logged off and headed to the bathroom to release some stress. That dude had better be hot. I swear if he turned out to be some catfishin' hillbilly. . . .

Adventure of a Lifetime

I finished training my last client around 5:45 p.m. and then went home to grab a quick bite to eat and a shower before heading downtown. On edge didn't begin to explain what I was feeling about the whole thing. I had no clue what this dude looked like. My instincts told me he'd be hot, since his body was nice, but he could be a total Daniel Craig. Everything is tasty but that face. I've had a few hookups where dude's body was bangin' but his face looked like roadkill. Bending a guy over the back of a chair, couch, or facedown on a bed meant I ain't hafta see his face too much. It was cool, though. You don't need to be smokin' to have a nice-size cock, toned ass, and talented mouth.

I took the train to Union Square and then caught a cab over to the Grand Royal—it was faster than taking the train all the way downtown. When I got to the hotel, it was about five minutes to eight. Taking in my surroundings, I was pretty shocked at the place Vinnie chose for us. Classy as fuck, and most definitely not someplace to bring a hookup. Someone I was trying to impress? Yeah. Someone I'd likely never see again? Hell nah, but it was his dime.

I headed straight for the elevators and entered when the doors parted. I pressed the button for the seventeenth floor before glancing over at an older couple who were also getting on the elevator. The lady, who I assumed was the guy's wife, was nagging him about drinking too much at dinner and the alcohol messin' with his medication. Wasn't my intention to eavesdrop, but I couldn't help it. Listening to their conversation damn near had me in stitches. You could tell they'd been together for years, since their bickering seemed to come naturally. The husband had a look on his face that said he'd rather be anywhere but in this elevator listening to his wife chew his ass out. I leaned against the panel and snickered at the guy's poor attempt to tune the woman out by staring at his phone.

Would I ever have that kind of bond with someone? Would someone ever care enough about me and my well-being to call me out on my behavior?

Staring at them reminded me of how much I wanted to be in a real relationship, but it wasn't the time to worry about that. This wasn't about romance. I was there for a drink, and if I was lucky, some head or a fuck. When the elevator doors opened on the tenth floor, the couple nodded in my direction before exiting. Moments later, I arrived on the seventeenth floor.

Time for some action.

Once I stepped off the elevator, I made my way down the hallway before stopping in front of the door marked 1709. I took a deep breath, knocked, and waited, a little nervous but nothin' out of the ordinary. Shit, I was too busy prayin' the guy was decent-looking more than anything. I *really* wanted to get a nut out of the night. Instead of Vinnie coming to the door to greet me, I heard a voice yell, "Come in!"

Not a good look. Dude couldn't even open the door? What was that about? He too good to come and greet me?

Like it was beneath him or some shit. Yeah, my gut told me something was off. You know when the tiny hairs on the back of your neck stand up? Like you know some bad shit is about to go down? I kinda had that feeling, but I was gonna see this through. Let somebody come at me the wrong way, they'd end up gettin' their ass beat.

I turned the knob tentatively and entered the hotel room. I was primed and ready to take out anyone and everyone in case this was some sort of shady-ass ambush. With people you met on the web, you just never know what to expect. He seemed okay online, but in person, who knew what the real deal was? Was the dude up to some fishy shit? Why bother to invite someone to your hotel room but not even open the door to greet them? Suspicious for sure.

"Hey, come on in, Manny." The voice came from further inside the room, close but not close enough. The lighting was turned down low. I couldn't see much other than the outline of a cream-colored sofa off to the far left and a couple of skyscrapers through the partially open curtains.

"Vinnie, where are you?" I yelled, inching the door closed. I didn't close it all the way. There was no way I was moving another goddamn inch without Vinnie showing his face. I was annoyed and starting to get pissed. This motherfucker was rude as hell.

"You ask me to have a drink, but you can't even greet me? What kinda crap is that?"

"Manny, close the door."

"Nah, man. Where are you? This is mad suspect. Why are you hiding? What's going on?"

A little voice in my head was screaming at me to get the fuck out of dodge, but nope, my dumb ass stood rooted to the spot near the door.

"Manny, I need you to close the door first, please. I need to know you're alone." His voice was bass-filled and strangled. Pleading. Shit might've been sexy if the entire scenario didn't seem sketchy as fuck.

What did he mean he "needed" me to close the door? Weird.

Curiosity had my common sense in a headlock. All the signs were telling me I shoulda bailed. Why would he think I wasn't alone? Was he expecting me to roll with a gang-bang entourage?

His request was odd but I could kinda understand. My best guess was that he was as unsure about me as I was of him. I'd make a good faith effort, but don't think I wasn't ready to take him out if he tried to gank me. Dude wasn't about to get the upper hand on me.

"All right. I'll close the door, but I'm not moving another inch until you show your face. And of course I'm alone. Who the hell would I bring?"

I closed the door to the hotel room and leaned against it, waiting for Vinnie to appear . . . and yo, nothing could've prepared me for what happened next.

"Vinnie" came into my line of sight a few seconds later. "Vinnie" was otherwise known as Christopher Kaine, television actor. Motherfuckin' *Christopher Kaine*! I wanted to freak out, but disbelief, anger, and horniness were all wrapped up in a ball of emotions.

He was my beer buddy for the evening? Nah, this had to be some kind of mistake. No way. No way. *No fucking way.*

You coulda knocked me the fuck over with a feather. You see, Christopher starred in the critically acclaimed and true-to-life television show *Blue Law*, on one of the top cable networks. This dude probably had pussy thrown at him from every direction, and he was gay. Gay. Gay. GAY.

Once the shock wore off, anger rose to the forefront as the dominant emotion. This shit was unreal.

"You can't be fuckin' serious!" I yelled. "Is this some kind of joke? Am I being Punk'd?" I'm pretty sure I was foaming at the mouth because dude had me vexed.

"I can explain," he said, holding up his hands. "Calm down, Manny. Relax and hear me out."

Calm down? Hear him out? Heck no, I wanted *out*. I didn't sign up for this and wanted no part of it. Why was *this* guy trolling a kinky website? He had crazy money. He couldn't afford an escort? I had too many questions, but now I wasn't entirely sure I wanted all of the answers. No, scratch that. I was *certain* I ain't want answers. This was going to get complicated real fast, and I wasn't interested in complications. It was time to bounce. I didn't know what the deal was, and it was probably best I stayed clueless.

"Nah, bro, I don't wanna know. I'm out." In my nervousness, I ended up fumbling with the doorknob just trying to get the damned thing open. When I finally managed to crack the door, Vinnie rushed over and slammed it shut all while pressing his body across my back. *How the fuck did he move so fast?*

"Please," he whispered against the back of my neck. His breath tickled the tiny hairs, giving me gooseflesh. "Don't go. Can you give me a minute to explain?"

I ain't gonna lie, his breath against my neck didn't just make the hairs on my arms and neck stand up, it also gave me a tingling sensation in my groin. I might have been pissed, but my dick was pretty cool with the situation. Fuckin' traitor.

I shrugged him off and turned to face him head on. He held up his hands and backed away, giving me space. Smart move, because crowding me when I was pissed was a bad idea.

Vinnie's . . . er, Christopher's eyes held so much sadness. For a split second I felt bad for all the shit he probably went through on a daily basis. To be under a microscope must be a nightmare. It was all summed up in the look he gave me. I didn't want his guilt. I knew that look. That was the look I had with Joulie. The one where all the shit you'd been trying to suppress clawed its way up your belly, making you look like you're swallowing vomit—glassy-eyed and pale. And it's all because you know what people will think if they found you out. It's the look I have when I think about telling Juan I'm bi. I immediately broke eye contact. No. I wasn't getting sucked into his mess. I didn't sign up for any pity party, and frankly, I was heated 'cause I got caught up in some bullshit.

He had better get to explaining, and fast. I followed him into the suite and he took a seat on one of the sofas. I chose to sit across from him in a wingback chair. On the low, I was scoping everything out. I tried to be as cool as possible about my surroundings, but the hotel room was impressive. Okay, the room was sick! I'd never seen anything so fancy in my life. I was pretty sure the price tag to stay here for a night was equivalent to a month of my own rent. Hell, maybe even more. I worked for rich people, but I never hung out with them. We weren't chill like that. I trained them and we went our separate ways. Hanging out with clients outside of work wasn't happening. They stayed with their kind and I stayed with mine. The line was invisible but clear as day. Needless to say, me ending up in a fancy hotel room with a gay TV star was about as out of my league as I could get. The entire situation was so fuckin' out of my league. *This* was why my dating life was shit. I couldn't seem to ever catch a break.

"You want a beer?" he asked, grabbing the bottle of Blue Moon off the coffee table. Those ridiculous electric blue eyes of his zeroed in on me. Maybe I was totally overanalyzing shit, but he looked kind of scared, as if he was trying just as hard as I was to hold it together and stay cool.

"Nah, I'm good. Not much in the mood for drinking anymore. You've got five minutes, *Vinnie*," I replied. I'm pretty sure he could pick up on the acidity that laced my words. Wasn't like I was trying to hide a damned thing.

He glanced at me again before homing in on his beer and then peeling away the label on the bottle.

After a few more moments of us sitting in uncomfortable silence and him picking at that damn label, he finally spoke. "You're pissed. I get it."

I slowly drew in a few deep breaths. "Nah dude, I don't think you do. I came here to toss back a few brews and maybe get my dick sucked."

"That's still on the table, Manny," he replied with a silly grin. "I had a feeling you'd be hot. Glad I wasn't wrong about that."

There wasn't shit to grin about. I didn't care that he found me attractive—okay, maybe I cared a little, but that wasn't the point.

"No, it's not. You're messy, Christopher. Yeah, *Christopher*." I watch MFN for the fights and *SportsTalk*, but I've caught a few episodes of *Blue Law*. It's a dope show, and once in a while, my TV will end up on *TMZ*, *Entertainment Tonight*, or one of those other bullshit celebrity shows. "I'm not stupid. I know exactly who you are."

"Okay," he replied softly.

I shook my head. "What are you doing? You have mad money. More money than I'll ever see in my lifetime. Why didn't you just hire an escort? At your level, why bother with hookup websites? You're in the closet. Hell, I'm kinda in the closet too, but I'm more out than you. The shit you're doing is messy and, honestly, I want no part of it. Can't nothin' good come out of this.

"There's gotta be some kind of service you can use. They'll sign a confidentiality agreement or somethin', and you get what you want."

He abruptly stood and slammed the bottle down on the table, which made beer splatter everywhere. Whoa, where'd that come from? Dude needed to relax.

"And that's the problem. Confidentiality agreements kill the mood. Who wants to fuck with a threat hanging over them? What kind of life is that? I'm no pedophile, yet I'm pretty sure I'd be treated like I am one . . . like I'm some kind of deviant with disgusting desires. It's 2016, and I still have to hide my sexuality because it could destroy my career.

"I'm an actor. A fairly famous and closeted actor. There's no way I can date without people hounding me, so forget about ever having a relationship. Indulging in anything kinky? Ha, right. My career would be over in a matter of hours. My contract with Movie Film Network could end from the scandal alone. Despite my lawyers going through it with a fine-toothed comb, if it got out that I like my sex a little less vanilla, and with a man, I have no doubt their lawyers would find a clause to nullify everything I've worked my ass off for. I know it. Hollywood likes to pretend they're accepting, but being gay is tolerated as long as you keep your personal business out of the spotlight. Being out works for Neil Patrick Harris, Zachary Quinto, and Matt Bomer, but name one out gay actor with a lead character on a Primetime television series. Comedy doesn't count. I'm talking about a TV show where the chemistry between the leading man and the leading lady is off the charts. And movies? What blockbuster has a gay male headlining? Sure they're side characters and behind the scenes, directing and writing the material, but none are in front of the camera."

Chris spoke through gritted teeth and clenched his fists. The fear in his eyes from earlier had turned to fire, and was now glowing embers of pain and frustration.

His voice quavered as he continued his tirade. "I live a lie every goddamn day. Every. Single. Day, Manny. Tonight I wanted something for myself. I wanted someone who wasn't trying to push me out of the closet and was fine with fooling around. You seemed like you'd be fun and into it. It was a bonus that you wanted a no-strings thing too. You also emphasized discretion was big for you. I need to be discreet, Manny. I need . . . I need to be free."

Leaning forward in the chair, I let out a long breath and ran my hands over my scalp. Shit was deep. I couldn't imagine being in Christopher's situation. I may not have been out to everyone, but at least I had some form of a support system who didn't give a fuck about who I slept with as long as I used protection and took precautions. Living that kind of lie had to be hell. I sympathized with him, but I was still fuckin' pissed I got dragged into this wreck.

I pressed my forearms against my knees, clasping and unclasping my hands. "I gotta ask. How are you free if you're living a lie? That ain't free.

"Pretending to be something you're not is asking for a shitload of trouble. It may not matter to you, but somewhere along the line you've probably hurt a lot of people pretending, Christopher. This is real life. Feelings are real. People are out here looking for love, and you shit on it by pretending. Man up, be yourself."

Even I was surprised by what came out of my mouth. I felt like a fraud. *Pot, meet the asshole kettle.* Here I was telling him to man up and own his shit, but I hid a part of myself from a woman I dated for over a year. I hid shit from my baby brother, my blood. The irony was too funny.

Christopher paced back and forth in front of the table. "How can you can tell me to be myself when you hide just as much as I do. Be myself? Okay, this from the guy who trolls a website for like-minded kinky professionals. Looking for discreet hookups isn't exactly manning up, is it?"

If looks could kill, that motherfucker woulda been dead on the spot. It's like he knew all about Joulie and Juan and was calling me out. What was he, a damn mind reader?

"We both live lies, Manny. You're not as free as you think. Don't sit there and act as if you're better than me.

"Holier than thou doesn't look good on you. It doesn't look good on anybody. We've all got secrets."

I stood to leave, forcing myself not to look at his body, so I focused on being annoyed and avoided acknowledging his partially clothed state. He leaned against the edge of the sofa, bare-chested and scowling. Christopher without a shirt was a problem. There was no denyin' it was difficult actin' like I didn't give a shit when all I kept thinking of was lickin' a path up his torso. His abs were on full display, and I swear to God the dude was subtly flexing, taunting me. *Oh, it's like that?*

I tried not to look, but every time I glanced around the room to focus on something, anything, to run interference, my eyes went right back to his chest and traveled down his abs and landed on his trim waist. He was different than The Architect, better. That guy was brawny, solid, wide. Christopher was lean with broad shoulders, a long torso, flat abs, and what was likely an insanely low percentage of body fat. Muscles minus the bulk. An image of my tongue swirling over his hipbone and following the dusting of fine hair that traveled from his navel and disappeared into his sweatpants came to mind. Not that I was payin' close attention or anything.

Man, he was handsome as fuck. Lookin' like a blond-haired, blue-eyed Nordic god. Christopher knew he was hot, and he caught me checkin' him out. My guess, he was getting off on it. Shame that this didn't turn out the way we both wanted. We could've had a good time. This would be the last fucking time I used kinkysinglesconnect to find some cock. Good ole reliable Grindr would have to suffice next time I was looking for a quickie. I'd take douchebags over drama any day.

Christopher walked past me and made his way over to the mini-fridge next to the bar, grabbing another beer.

"You sure you don't want one?" he asked while carelessly popping the cap off his beer.

"Nah. I'm good. I'm gonna bail, but you should probably clean this mess up," I said, pointing to the spill on the table. The words came out of my mouth, but again, my feet made no effort to move me toward the door. I wanted to leave. My mind was screaming to get the hell out, but I stood there paralyzed.

How would I play this? Cool and unaffected or pissed? My sole reason for being in that hotel was to get off. This was more than I had bargained for, and I wasn't gonna get a nut outta the whole ordeal. Still, my damn feet wouldn't move.

Christopher must have picked up on my unease and confusion. He eyed me and took a swig of beer before heading to take a seat on the sofa, leaving me standing like an idiot by the bar and tasting his cologne in the air. He sat down, his body slumping against the cushions while he took another drink. I couldn't stop staring. Why couldn't I just forget about the lying and make the best of the circumstances? When would I ever get the chance to mess around with a celebrity again? Anyone else in my situation woulda been eatin' this up, but my dumb ass was too caught up in being mad.

It wasn't until I watched Christopher get comfortable that I realized that if I left now, I'd be missin' out on a damn good opportunity, a once-in-a-lifetime kinda deal. This shit was like hitting PowerBall.

The sweatpants Christopher wore slid down his hips as he pressed himself deeper into the cushions. Each time he shifted, the sweatpants eased down more until they were barely hanging on. One wrong—or right—move and he'd be out of 'em. *Dude, come on. No fair.*

I cleared my throat. "I'll, uh . . . catch you later," I said, finally making a move toward the door.

"Wait!" he called out.

I turned, looking over my shoulder. "What?"

For the love of God, all I wanted to do was blow a fuckin' load, but this was the opening act to a shit show.

"You don't have to do anything, just watch. Sit and watch me, Manny. Don't leave. You're trying to save face, but I know you don't want to go. Stay and watch me for a bit."

I let out a chuckle. "What makes you think I wanna watch?" I said, meeting his eyes. Those stupid, hypnotic, gorgeous blue eyes of his. Now I knew what women meant when they said they really dug my eyes. This dude was perfect. Absolutely perfect, and my dick thought so too.

He set his beer down on the table. "You're here, aren't you?" he replied, shoving his right hand into his sweatpants, fondling his dick. "You wouldn't have come tonight if you weren't interested in me."

Coño.

"If you want to join me instead of watching, I won't stop you," he said, his voice low and husky. Shit was sexy but I had to be one step ahead of his ass.

"And what's preventing me from walking out that door right now, calling every tabloid under the sun, and tellin' them you propositioned me for sex?"

He stopped all movement and stared up at me, his jaw muscles clenching. Damn, I might've played that hand all wrong.

"You don't want to. I get that you're pissed at me, Manny, but you don't want to do that. For what? Out of spite? Do you really want to end everything I've worked hard for because I didn't come clean?

"Let's face it, if you out me, it also means admitting *you* enjoy being with men. Are you ready to be out? How quickly we forget, *TrainerBoy*. So that's what's stopping you from 'calling every tabloid under the sun.' You ruin me, you ruin yourself. But I don't get the asshole vibe from you. Or am I mistaken?"

I tightened my fists and my face went neutral, not giving any hints to whether or not he was right. I had no fear of coming out. Or did I? I mean, I hadn't told anyone but my moms and Titi Lucia that I was bi. Hell, even my brother had no clue. Joulie didn't know I identified as bisexual, but I was never with a guy while she and I were together. I was monogamous throughout our entire relationship, but still, I never told her I was bisexual, and I should've.

Maybe I was afraid. Maybe I thought she'd judge me, look at me differently. Maybe I cared too much about what other people would think. Double standards and all. Chicks can totally identify as bi without the stigma, but guys? Nah, not so much. We get pegged as being confused, deceitful, conniving, diseased, femmy, or whateva. I didn't deceive Joulie, not in the way people might think. I know for a fact I would've told her if she was *my one*. I didn't do anything to jeopardize our relationship. I was faithful, I just . . . well, I held back a big part of myself from her. No real surprise we didn't work out. Hiding things from your partner was no way to establish anything lasting, right? Guess I didn't develop any deep feelings because I sabotaged the relationship from the beginning.

Christopher quirked his brow, studying me. He was pretty calm for a guy whose career I just threatened to end.

"You want to end everything for me right now? Go ahead, be an asshole. But that guilt will stay with you for life. I hope you enjoy the rewards in that closet of yours. Don't think you're the fucking hero here, Manny," he spat out. "You're not that different from me, not by a long shot."

Well, would you look at that. When backed into a corner, looked like Mr. MFN had a temper. Good, then we were fuckin' even.

"Are you done?" I asked. Despite the flaring tempers on both ends, I found a pissed-off Christopher intensely hot. The way his eyes bore into me definitely said he wanted to slug me. I stirred up some shit, and it was pretty damn enticing. He wasn't backing down. I didn't think for a minute he could take me, but I'd like to see him try. My dick twitched at the thought of me grinding against Christopher with him at my mercy. Yeah, that was one nice image.

He answered me with a grunt, and I ambled over to reclaim my spot in the wingback.

"Pull 'em down," I demanded. No sweet nothings between lovers whispered here. This was gonna be dirty. Fuck all the nonsense, my dick was aching and I wanted to come. Hate sex tended to reap some impressive orgasms. He was mad at me. I was furious with him. This shit needed to happen *now*.

With a twinkle in his eyes, he hurriedly obeyed my command. Still the good little sub despite being pissy. The fact that he liked being told what to do could work to my advantage. If he wanted a "beefy Dominant" he was gonna get what he asked for.

Christopher pulled the sweatpants down his hips, and his curved cock jutted upward. Gotta say, the outline from his selfie didn't do him justice. Just as he said, he was uncut—exactly how I liked 'em—and that got a grin outta me. His cock was short and fat, about six and a half inches, but I had no real idea until I was able to get a closer look. Trust me, I wanted to explore. Didn't matter that he didn't have length, he was thick. I liked thick. Goddamn, I was getting excited just thinkin' about playing with his dick.

I fumbled to unbutton my pants, and then I pulled my dick out above the waistband of my underwear, flinching when the elastic touched my nuts. I was already sportin' impressive wood, but I hadn't yet reached my full potential. Christopher's eyes landed on my cock before his gaze traveled up my body and locked with mine. I watched him watchin' me. The fire was still there but he looked more than ready to take whatever I decided to dish out.

I spat on my hand for a bit of lubrication before gripping my cock, pumping my shaft up and down at a steady pace. Christopher let out a groan as he did the same to his own fat cock. Shit, what a sight. I saw why he was a big deal.

On TV he was what women's dreams were made of. The taut, suave, single police detective looking for love after the murder of his fiancée. His character was loved by millions, many of them undoubtedly women. But right now he sat in front of me. *Me*. Stroking his dick, staring at me, eyes filled with need and pent-up sexual tension.

Precum built up as I continued strokin' my shaft. *This would've been even better with lube . . . or if it was his hand instead of mine.*

My breathing hitched like I was bustin' out bicep curls as I pumped my dick faster, my hips gyrating upward to meet the thrust of my hand. I slapped my erect cock against my stomach and abruptly stopped. I didn't want to come yet; I wanted more. I *needed* more. I deserved more for this bullshit inconvenience. My eyes were glued to Christopher. *Damn this*. Enough with the mutual jacking off. I wanted to get what I was promised. I wanted to shoot my load down some lover boy's throat, and he was the winner.

I toed off my shoes and socks before pulling off my jeans and staggering over to stand in front of Christopher without bothering to take my shirt off. I was far more concerned with getting my dick in his mouth. He looked up at me, tightly gripping his cock. Those stupid blue eyes shining brightly.

"Open up," I ordered.

Leaning forward, Christopher happily obliged and opened his mouth, granting my cock entrance into what had to be the softest place on this motherfuckin' earth.

"Fuuuuck. Damn."

I'm a bit above average, about eight inches long, and got a bit of girth goin' on. Never had any complaints about not being able to satisfy, that's for sure, but he took all of me on the first try. He deep-throated like a champ, and I felt the head of my cock tickling the back of his throat. I immediately tensed. Guys who could take me fully without gaggin' were always a weakness, and Christopher wasn't any different. His enthusiasm was admirable. This had to have been the first bit of action he'd experienced in a long while. Pretty fucked up. No sense in worrying about shit that had no direct impact on me, but leading a closeted life pretty much ensured a garbage sex life.

"Get on your knees," I mumbled while my hands slid through his soft blond hair. He obeyed my command, lowering his body from the sofa and onto the floor to kneel in front of me. His hands rested against my thighs as his tongue teased and taunted me, swirling around the head of my cock. *That mouth!*

"Uhh . . . ohhh, so good. Feels fuckin' incredible," I said, gripping locks of Christopher's hair. He did this thing where he would slowly lick the head of my dick, alternating between tonguing the slit and creating crazy suction that rivaled a good Fleshlight—borderline painful but hella pleasurable, and the hottest fuckin' thing.

You know what made the whole scenario unbelievable? No hands. Dude bobbed up and down on my dick with that greedy mouth of his without using his hands. Well, he *used* his hands—his fingers dug into my ass, pullin' me deeper into his mouth. His warm breath tickled my pubes right before he nibbled on my balls. He flattened his tongue, licking back and forth over the underside of my nuts, driving me crazy. Christopher rapidly jerked his cock while his tongue went back to toying with the head of my dick and probing my slit. He opened wide, stuffing both of my balls in his mouth. Holy shit, he was giving head like a porn star, so damn enthusiastic, suckin' my cock like it was his job and he was about to have a massive payday.

"Lick those balls like a good little cock slut. You like licking my nuts, huh? Show me you like sucking me off. Take that dick. Suck it, suck it hard."

He looked up at me just before releasing my balls and taking me whole, his eyes full of lust. His nose nestled in my pubic hair, and my hands gripped the back of his head as I thrust my hips forward, not caring about his comfort level while I roughly fucked his face. His breathing sped up each time he tried to inhale between thrusts. The faster he bobbed his head, the more I pushed him down onto my dick. The hollowing of his mouth and the suction on my cock was in-fuckin-sane. Christopher pulled back, and I looked down to see a mix of drool and precum dangling from his lips. So fuckin' sexy.

"Does it taste good? You like having this big juicy dick in your mouth?"

He responded by delivering a trail of kisses along my abdomen before suckling my nuts. I shuddered.

"Your balls are so full," he whispered.

He wasn't lyin', my balls were unbelievably heavy. There was a spot right underneath my left nut that could get me to blow in like a second. As soon as my partner put the right amount of pressure there with their tongue, I could come in record time. I loosened my grip and eased his head off my dick because at this rate, my load was about to ooze down the back of his throat if he hit that spot one more time. It was what I wanted to happen for sure, but not so fast. On the other hand, Christopher seemed like he was pretty close to bustin' a nut. He tugged and stroked his cock with his right hand like a madman, all while the fingernails of his left hand dug into the flesh of my ass cheek.

He tenderly kissed the head of my dick and it was nearly my undoing. I forced my dick back into his mouth. I never wanted his lips to leave my cock.

"Shit . . . that's it, take my cock. Take it all. Suck that dick, suck it."

Christopher let out an affirmative groan. Gotta give credit where it's due, the dude was seriously skilled. If Dick-Sucking 101 were a college course, he would definitely be the instructor. He was up there with my top three best blow jobs ever. His tongue traveled up and down my shaft, licking every single vein. Fuck. I could feel that tingling sensation stirring in the pit of my stomach. He picked up the pace, and his head bobbed faster up and down on my dick. His lips tightened around the head of my cock and created just the right amount of pressure.

"Jesus! Shit, you keep that up, and I ain't gonna last."

"Mmm," he moaned.

"Is that what you want? You want me to come in your mouth? Hungry for my cum, cock slut?"

Instead of answerin', Christopher lifted up off my dick and started jerking my cock at a rapid pace. His mouth open wide waiting for my seed to hit its target.

"Ungh. Fuck, here it comes. Here it comes!"

With my fingers tangled in his hair, my sticky load landed everywhere: on his chin, on his cheek, on his nose, some even managed to make it into his mouth. I missed his eye by an inch or so. My orgasm was pretty fuckin' powerful; you'd think I hadn't beat off in the shower last night. There was so much cum. Christopher licked my cum from his lips and my dick. I needed to get him a towel. My jizz sploshing all over his face was hot to me, but probably not the most appealin' thing to him. We never discussed facials, but hell, there wasn't any need to now.

My lips parted in a wide grin as I looked down into those bedroom blues of his. He was the type of dude where all it would take was one look and you'd be done for. I got that vibe. He was too fuckin' attractive for his own good. I let go of his head and took a step back, bending to grab my jeans. I pulled them on and zipped up while Christopher leaned back on his haunches and watched me. I couldn't help but stare at those thick, sinewy thighs of his. Perfect. Damn . . .

TV star, many women's dream man, and most definitely the star of many a gay fantasy, Christopher Kaine, just sucked my dick. Talk about a surreal moment.

Dead air was not about to overshadow my dope-ass orgasm, so I cut the tension. No crushin' my high. "You sure do got a purty mouth," I said with my best Southern twang.

Still on his knees and with a face full of cum, Christopher laughed. "Funny, real funny."

I smiled and then headed down the hall in search of the bathroom. Once I found the right door, I quickly grabbed a towel and made my way back to the living room area of the suite. I tossed the towel to Christopher, who was rising from the carpeted floor.

Well, now that that was over, I wasn't sure what came next, but I didn't want to overstay my welcome. I leaned down to slip on my kicks and grab my underwear, shoving them, along with my socks, into my back pocket. I'd wait until I got to the lobby to use the restroom and clean up before heading back uptown. My goal was to be easy about what just happened and inch myself toward the door.

"Well Christopher, uh, yeah . . . that was cool. I appreciate the blow job, man. You have an amazing mouth. Badass skills." Fuckin' understatement of the century. "I'm gonna head out. You take care of yourself and stay gold."

The faster I bailed, the less opportunity guilt trips, pity parties, and eventually, regret had to work with. Shit was awkward as fuck, but hot. Yep, I was rude. Christopher hadn't gotten off; I shoulda offered to reciprocate. But Christopher also had mad baggage. Even though one of the entertainment industry's most eligible bachelors had my cum drying on his face, I wasn't interested in hanging around. I had my own issues, but it ain't like I was carrying the weight of the world on my shoulders, which seemed to be the case for him. I would end this little correspondence on my terms and leave with some fuckin' pep in my step.

The look Christopher gave me was very different from the lustful one from a few seconds ago when he was wiping my spunk off his cheek. "So, that's it? I suck you off and you leave? End of story?"

"Sure. I mean, what else did you expect? I *was* on my way out before you begged me to stay. None of this went down the way it should've, with the exception of the head I just got."

"You can't be serious. I expected to get fucked. I suck you, you fuck me. A little quid pro quo, Manny. Don't tell me you're one of those selfish types who's only the recipient but never reciprocates. Get the fuck over it already. I left out some information. I'm sorry, jeez. You blew off some steam, so now it's my turn."

Someone calling me on my shit was funny to me. I was totally one of those types. Christopher saw right through me and, sure as shit, didn't mince words when it came to what he wanted. I liked that.

"So there's some truth to me calling you a cock slut after all. You're jonesin' for a fuck. You want my dick that bad, huh? Everyone has you pegged all wrong."

He tossed the towel onto the sofa. "That's why you shouldn't make assumptions about people. What you think you know isn't always accurate," he countered in a smartass tone.

At least the *come mierda* didn't sound like he regretted anything. Christopher's arrogance made me feel a hell of a lot better.

He moved toward me and leaned in close before grabbing my hips, his breath warm against my face. "First of all, call me Chris. Christopher is way too formal considering I just swallowed your cum." His lips found the perfect spot on my neck and he licked a path back and forth between my jaw and earlobe. "Second, yes, I do want it that bad. I want you pounding into me. It's been a long while since I've been with someone, Manny." His hands wound their way around my neck as he looked into my eyes. "You're hot, and I want you inside me. The blow job was just a sample of what's to come."

Shhhhhit. Dude *was* in a dick drought. Sayin' he wanted me inside him made my dick swell. Forget that I just came, I was ready to go again.

"Why me? I still can't wrap my head around any of this."

"You ask too many questions," he said, grabbing my hand and leading me down the hall toward the bedroom. My underwear and socks fell out of my back pocket and landed somewhere between the bedroom and the living room area, but I didn't even care. He let go of my hand to open the French doors to the bedroom, and I forgot how to breathe for a sec. I let out a low whistle, taking in my surroundings while Chris ducked into the master bath. This shit couldn't be real. The bed was huge; the television mounted on the wall was gigantic. The couches, the chairs, the ridiculous amount of space was crazy. I'd never been exposed to this kind of shit in my life. The nicest hotel room I'd ever been in was the Sheraton in New Orleans when me and my crew decided to rent an Escalade and do a road trip for Mardi Gras. That was six of us packed into a room that held two king-size beds. This here was some next-level shit.

Chris came out of the bathroom and headed toward the bed. "Just so you know, I don't bareback. I have condoms and lube," he murmured, rifling through a drawer of the nightstand. He closed the drawer after removing a few condoms and a bottle of lubricant.

I was barely listenin' to what came out of his mouth because I was so hypnotized by the view of the Hudson River. This room had to come with a ridiculous price tag for access to a view like that. Could we be more different? Him: famous, rich white dude. Me: Latino entrepreneur who stocked up on ramen noodles and peanut butter when Key Food had a sale. This dude was so beyond my scope, but he didn't act any different from a hookup I would've scored downtown at one of the gay bars in Chelsea.

Honestly, I didn't know if taking this shit to the next level with Christopher was a good thing or a bad thing. I held my own. I had my own business and made money legitimately doing shit I loved. Some days were a struggle, and I fell on hard times every now and again, but I woke up with a sense of purpose. Maybe I was overthinking things. I knew this was just about sex, but I couldn't help but wonder if I was some sort of pity fuck or Chris had a Latino fetish. He seemed genuinely attracted to me, but you know, there's always somebody on the web lookin' to get their rocks off with that token piece of ass.

I needed to stop with the assumptions and just take the moment for what it was, because an opportunity like this wouldn't ever happen again.

Stayin' in my head was gonna fuck everything up, so I focused on the twinkling lights near the waterfront seventeen stories down. "Good, I don't bareback either. If rubbers aren't required, we ain't fuckin'. Seems like it's a little too late to be having this discussion, but I'm clean. I get tested every six weeks. Got a copy of my results in my wallet if you wanna see."

He raised an eyebrow. "Every six weeks? Sleep around a lot?"

I laughed, pulling off my polo. "I like sex. I like safe sex. I like to be certain I stay safe, so if that means gettin' tested more often, I'm cool with that."

"I'm cool with it too," Chris replied, his eyes focusing on my tattoos. "I haven't had sex with anyone in a few months, and my last test was negative. Like you said, it's a little too late to be having this discussion, but I'll take a look at your results. I can have my assistant email my last physical including all blood work if you want."

"Yeah, have your assistant send those over. Better to be safe than sorry. And what do you mean by a few months?" I said, reaching into the pocket of my jeans for my wallet. At least that hadn't fallen out too.

"Seventeen," he whispered, avoiding eye contact. He left the bedroom and headed back into the living room area, returning shortly and typing on his phone.

"She's always attached to her phone. I get what I pay for. Give me a sec, and she'll send all of my medical history. I'll pull up my last STI panel and get you what you want." He pressed a few buttons on his phone, and about two minutes later, he handed his phone over to me.

"There are my results."

I took the phone, but I was still stuck on what he said before he went into the other part of the suite.

Delayed reaction for real. "Wait, wait, wait. Hold up. You haven't had sex in seventeen months, and tonight you decide you want to? And with me? Why?"

I looked over the results dated well over a year ago, all displaying "Negative," before handing him his phone and the piece of paper with my test results. He looked them over and gave the paper back to me.

"So, Emmanuel Acosta, is it?"

"Manny," I corrected. "We're good on the tests," I said folding the paper and slipping it along with my wallet into my back pocket. "You're basically a born-again virgin at this stage, and no one calls me Emmanuel 'cept my little brother."

"Understood." Chris placed his phone on the nightstand, and I pulled off my sneakers and jeans, tossing my jeans onto a nearby chair. I was buck-ass naked.

The location of my underwear was suddenly a high priority. That delayed reaction was doin' a number on my ass. Everything finally sunk in. I was stark naked and on the verge of having a panic attack in this dude's bedroom. A fuckin' TV star who'd been celibate for seventeen months now wanted *me* to break the streak. I took a seat on the edge of the bed. Funny, I was cool with everything few minutes ago, but now I was getting antsy over the whole ordeal, and not in a good way.

Chris made his way over to where I was sitting and kneeled in front of me, placing the condoms and lube next to me on the bed. I admired his naked body on the low, but I'm pretty sure he could sense that I was about a second away from freakin' the fuck out. I took a couple of deep breaths, hoping that would help. I talked a good game, but this . . . this was a lot to take in.

He stroked his hands up and down my thighs. "You have an amazing body. Relax, Manny."

Chris stuck his tongue out and swirled it around my nipple before pulling back and looking up at me. Fuck, fuck, fuck.

"Why you? Why now? Tonight is about me letting go. I'm tired of pretending, Manny. All I want is to belong to someone, even if it's for a night. Is it a little sad? I guess, but it's been too long. I'm horny and lonely, and tonight I want that to change. A little male companionship and an orgasm that isn't courtesy of my hand is all I want out of this. No strings. You're attractive, and I'd like us to have some fun. We do this and go our separate ways if that's what you want."

So it was possible that this wouldn't be just a one-time thing. Okay, cool, but what was up with that shit about wanting to belong to someone? Like he rolled the dice and I was the lucky motherfucker for the night. "*Someone*? That how it works? I just happened to be online at the right time?"

"No, no that's not what I meant. But, yes, technically, I could've sparked up conversation with any guy on kinkysinglesconnect, but I wanted to talk to you. I liked your body. I liked your tattoos. I liked that you were discreet. I liked that you also wanted something without complications. I like the same things you find sexy, and I think we could have a good time together."

Okay, seemed simple enough. I could make this happen. I wanted this to happen. "So, here we are," I replied.

"Here we are," he echoed.

"I'm gonna warn you now, I just may be the best you ever had. Try not to hold it against me."

He met my eyes and laughed. Glad he thought it was funny, but I was dead-ass serious. If I only got one shot at this, I was gonna make sure he remembered tonight for a long while. My nerves were dissolving and I was gettin' back in the zone.

"The best, you say?"

"Yeah, I say."

We both paused for a moment to stare at each other. Neither of us was bold enough to make a move. If this was going to happen, I had to be the one to get the ball rollin'. He was hesitant. I thought it was because he was just as scared as I was, despite my cocky attitude. Couldn't say I blamed him. Funny how less than thirty minutes ago I was ready to bounce and never give this guy another thought, but now I was trying to calm us both down and get in the mood for some serious fucking.

My heartbeat amplified in my eardrums—I was really about to do this. I locked eyes with Chris, tilted my head, and leaned in close before I finally kissed him. My hands tangled in Chris's hair as my lips pressed against his mouth, coaxin' him to open up for me. He parted his lips slightly, and I snaked my tongue across them, nibbling before pressing my tongue inside his mouth, anxious to taste him. I couldn't believe this shit was happening.

Chris's flavor was a mixture of tart and salty, with a hint of sweet; my cum had something to do with that. His mouth was addictive. I pulled him in even closer, loving the smell of his clean, herbal, woodsy musk, mingled with sex that clung to his flesh. I broke the kiss, not exactly wanting to stop, but I was itchin' to bury my cock deep inside of him. I was so fuckin' hard. Chris said he wanted something with no strings attached. He wanted to get fucked? Happy to oblige. Tight-assed bottoms were a weakness, after all.

I pulled Chris up from the floor by his hair, forcing him onto the bed. He could've put up a fight, but even if he hadn't mentioned his fondness for "beefy Dominants" in his profile, I woulda spotted his submissiveness a mile away. Despite being two inches taller than me, he liked being manhandled, and I liked being in control. He lay on his stomach as I straddled his ass. I leaned down to take a bite, I couldn't resist, it was callin' me. He groaned and flinched before trying to scoot up the bed. Judging from his chiseled ass he sure as hell didn't miss many squat days. I was going to enjoy watching my dick slide between those firm cheeks. Mr. MFN had no idea what was comin' his way. He was about to get the fuckin' of his life. After seventeen months of celibacy, he deserved to feel the aftereffects of my dick for the next couple of days. Seventeen months? Hell nah. Ain't no way I'd go that long without sex.

I grabbed the lube and drizzled a bit down the crack of his ass. I also squirted a dollop onto two of my fingers before flipping the cap closed.

"Spread your legs," I ordered.

Chris quickly complied.

"You ain't gonna pull none of that power bottom shit, right?" I asked, gripping his ass cheek with my left hand.

He buried his face into one of the oversized pillows before answering me. "No. I always like to let the top set the mood. Um, considering it's been a long while, take it easy on me, okay? When I said I want you pounding into me, it was a figure of speech."

I chuckled. "Can't guarantee I won't wax that ass. You asked for a beefy Dominant type. Was just checkin' to see if that's what you really wanted. Next time, be careful what you ask for, Chris."

He turned and glanced at me over his shoulder, eyes wide. "Manny . . ."

"I'll try my best to go easy, but no guarantees," I said, letting my lubed up fingers gently brush across his hole. I did this a couple of times, tryna get Chris to relax. I kept all my movements slow and gentle before breaching his ass.

Chris's body bucked as he moaned. "Shit, ahhh . . . that feels good. Ungh . . ."

He pushed back against my fingers, so I added another. Soon, I was knuckles-deep in his ass. Stroking, prodding, driving him fuckin' crazy. Safe to say he was pretty damn aroused.

His body was perfect. The curves and ridges of Chris's lean muscles built up my excitement, and all that squirmin' as I stretched his ass made it tough to concentrate.

He may have been out of the game for a minute but he had an eager little hole. I moved my index finger upward, finally making contact with a chestnut-sized bump, his p-spot. He took a couple of frantic breaths in between groans. Pushing his ass further against my knuckle as I moved inside him, I made a come-hither motion, and Chris damn near jackknifed off the bed. It was like ridin' a bucking bronco or some shit. I eased up. If I kept this up, there was no doubt he was gonna come. Slowly, I thrust my fingers in and out of his ass, stimulating those lil fuckin' nerve endings surrounding his hole. Chris reached between his legs and started strokin' himself as he lay on his stomach. My weight pressing down on the back of his thighs made it hard for him to get access to his dick since he couldn't exactly reposition me.

"I can't wait to shove my dick into your tight hole and fuck this sweet ass," I said, delivering a hard slap to his ass cheek. "Fuck, Chris, you know how many guys would love to be in my position right now?

"Mmm."

He wasn't much of a talker. A groaner, sure. A moaner, definitely, but not a talker.

I slapped my cock against his ass when he tried to lift himself up. Then I slid off his thighs to give him room to maneuver up on all fours and back into me. My fingers went back to steadily plunging in and out of his hole, prepping him for my dick. Seventeen celibate months. I know I said I'd try to be easy, but he was gonna be tight. I just hoped *I* didn't come too fast.

"Look at you, you're hungry for me. You want a deep dickin', but I want you back on your stomach." I pressed down on the small of his back to entice him to lay flat.

"Ah, Manny, shit. Put on a condom and fuck me. I'm ready," he growled.

"You want this big cock fillin' that needy hole, huh?"

"Uhh-hnn." He tensed up a bit and grunted when I stuck my thumb in his ass. Chris lifted his ass up off the bed and gripped his cock, moving his hips back and forth as he stroked himself.

I withdrew my thumb and leaned back, grabbing one of the condoms from the foot of the bed. I tore the foil and quickly rolled the condom onto my dick. He chose the thin lubricated kind, nice. He was ready, I didn't need to add more lube, all I had to do was slide in.

I nudged Chris's legs apart and angled my dick between his ass cheeks. I inched forward, and with a light thrust of my hips, my dick found his entrance. He whimpered before arching his back and lifting his ass up to meet my thrust, and his pink puckered hole welcomed my invasion. The ring of muscle relaxed and I was able to push myself deeper inside him. His hole swallowed my dick and it felt amazing . . . so fuckin' satisfying.

When I was fully seated inside Chris, I laid my palms flat underneath his arms and we stilled for a minute. I rocked back and forth, gettin' used to the feel of him before I rode that fine ass. He grabbed the sheets as I drove my dick into him. For a minute, the anger I felt about him lyin' to me came back, and I focused all of that aggression into my hips, slamming into him. Never once did Chris complain about me bein' too rough. He was the perfect bottom, matchin' me stroke for stroke. The deeper I went, the higher he lifted his ass. The rougher I got, the more he accepted. We were sexually compatible so far, and I loved it. Shit, I loved fuckin' anyone—woman or man—who could tolerate my pace. I pushed Chris's face down into the sheets and let my full weight settle on his back. For better leverage, I lifted his arms and clasped my hands behind his neck, and then I crammed his asshole with every ounce of me, and he took it like a good boy.

"Oh fuck! Fuck me, Manny, fuck me."

"You like this dick? Tell me you like the way I'm fuckin' you."

"It's so fucking big . . . ohh . . . shit. I like it. God, I fucking like it."

Seventeen months was a long time. He had earned his pleasure, and I told him as much. *"Te lo has ganado. Diecisiete meses es mucho tiempo,"* I whispered against his ear.

I changed my position, and with my urging—more like me hurlin' his ass up—Chris followed my lead and got up on all fours. Once we were back in our groove, my nails dug into his skin, grippin' his waist tight as I fucked him doggy style. Chris was a snug fit. Yeah, he was tight, but that was expected.

"Push back and ride this dick. Ride it. Help me fuck that tight little ass."

I leaned over his shoulder and delivered sloppy kisses. I had never been much of a kisser with guys during sex, but the kiss Chris and I shared before I prepped his ass was nice. Not quite innocent. Not quite dirty, but nice. I liked it and made an effort to savor more of him.

"Turn over. I wanna see you," I said, pulling out so Chris could turn onto his back. Once he was on his back, he spread his legs wide and began to jerk himself off. I pulled him closer and leaned forward, gripping the base of my dick before reentering him. He groaned, and I grabbed his ankles once I was back in firm but comfortable quarters.

"Mmm, you like that?"

"Uh . . . yeah," he mumbled.

I leaned down to kiss him while he gripped his cock. He bit my lip, and that just egged me on.

"God, that feels so good, Manny, so . . . ahh."

I pulled out slowly and thrust back in, teasing him with my dick.

"Please—fuck—make me come."

I pinned Chris's legs back and slammed into him while he stroked his shaft. We had developed a rhythm. The harder I thrusted, the faster his hand moved up and down his shaft.

I looked down at his face, and it was the most beautiful fuckin' thing. Those blue eyes shinin' . . .

"Uh-ngh" was all I heard before jets of thick white cum streaked across Chris's chest. That shit was hot.

I pulled out and ripped the condom off, strokin' my cock at a frantic pace and I came all over Chris's dick.

After I came, I collapsed face-first on the bed and tried to catch my breath. My heart was pounding a mile a fuckin' minute like I'd been doin' a shit-ton of box jumps.

Rolling onto my back, I mumbled, "Jesus, that was fuckin' good."

A laugh and an "uh-huh," came from somewhere near my thigh. How the hell did he get down there? "It was more than good," he mumbled. "My body feels weird."

"That's usually a good sign, I think," I replied.

"If you asked me to get up and walk right now, I'm pretty sure my legs would give out. I have this humming sensation flowing through my body. You know how a rubber band gets when it's pulled tight? Like if you let it go, it'll propel itself into the stratosphere? That's what I feel like right now. Like any minute I'm going to bounce off the walls."

"That's your body's way of saying you just got some good dick," I said through a smile that was hidden underneath my arm slung across my face. "Told ya it would be the best you ever had."

"When's the last time you had sex with a guy before tonight?" he asked me, changing the subject.

What? He wasn't impressed by my stroke game? He sure as shit wasn't complaining while grindin' on my cock.

I hesitated, but what was the point in lying? He already knew I liked sex. Did this shit mean he was about to start psychoanalyzing me?

"Two days ago," I huffed out. "An old gym buddy from back in the day I mess with sometimes."

"You had sex forty-eight hours ago, and now you're in bed with me?"

"I can get up and leave since we're done. I was just taking a minute to catch my breath before I grabbed my shit and left."

Way to ruin the fuckin' moment.

"No, wait. That's not what I meant. I'm putting my foot in my mouth."

I heard him scampering up the bed to lay next to me. I moved my arm from my face to look over to him, and he laid there starin' at me.

"What?" I asked.

"I wasn't kicking you out, Manny. I'd actually like it if you stayed the night—I mean, that is, if you want to. I was just curious how long it's been since you were with a man. I shouldn't have asked since it's really none of my business. I guess . . . I didn't expect you to say two days ago, is all. You caught me by surprise."

"As long as you're not trying to scrutinize me or make me feel like shit for liking sex, it ain't a big deal."

"No, that's not my intention. I'm sorry, it came out the wrong way."

"It's cool. So, you want me to stay?" I said, staring into those blazing blue eyes of his. How the hell did his eyes get like that? They were so damn bright and kinda sexy. Dilated pupils and all.

"Yeah, if you're okay with that."

"You wanna fuck some more, huh? You're covered in jizz and already thinking about the next round?" I was feelin' kinda good that he asked me to stay. I don't usually spend the night, but we had a good thing here, and I wouldn't mind hittin' it a few more times. Might as well get in another nut while I could.

He laughed. "Well, yeah," he responded all bashful-like. "But if you'd rather leave, I understand."

"Never had this happen before," I blurted out, avoiding eye contact.

This was new shit for me. No dude had ever asked me to stay. But despite our rocky start, I liked Chris. I liked him enough to kiss him during sex. That *never* happened with a hookup.

I also never came that fuckin' hard from sex with a hookup. It's rare to vibe with someone on the first fuck, you know? Usually, shit got awkward fast, but aside from the whole *I'm a famous actor and sorry I didn't mention it* debacle, we meshed. When it came to sex, we were on the same page. But there was no way I'd see him again. Dude was an in-the-closet actor and I was a semi-closeted personal trainer from the Boogie Down. Two different lifestyles, two different classes, two different ethnic backgrounds. But I wasn't rollin' with any of that tonight.

"What do you mean you've never had this happen before?" he asked.

"You know, a situation where a guy asked me to spend the night."

"No?"

"No."

"Really?"

I rolled my eyes and folded my arms behind my head. "Yeah."

"Well, there's a first time for everything," he said before snaking down my body, taking my cock into his mouth.

"Oh . . . sh-sh-iiit."

———

That night was full of firsts. It was the first time Chris and I fucked, it was also the first time I ever spent the night with a guy after a fuck. We ended up having sex twice more that night before finally passing out. My dick felt like I had been rubbing it against sandpaper, but it was worth it. When I woke the next morning, my arm was trapped underneath Chris's pillow. His back was turned to me, so I tried to be stealthy and extract my arm, which was basically numb. That pins-and-needles feeling wasn't nothin' nice. After maneuvering into some weird-ass positions that woulda made a contortionist proud, I was able to get out of bed.

I was shaking my arm, tryna get the blood circulating again, when Chris shifted under the covers. I stopped moving. The view of the Hudson was even better with the sun shining, which was helping to put me in a bright mood considering my arm was basically actin' like a paperweight. Despite gettin' up at the crack of dawn every day, I have never been a morning person. But this morning I was on my way toward being giddy as fuck. I'd had crazy monkey sex with Christopher Kaine. All. Goddamn. Night. I didn't wanna make shit awkward for either of us, so I hobbled over to the chair in the corner of the bedroom and pulled on my jeans and picked my shirt up off the floor. I put it on quick but realized I should've waited until I got to the living room since I still needed to find my underwear. Just as I was about to look for my drawers, he spoke.

"Leaving?" he asked.

I immediately tensed up.

Busted. No sense in tryna act like I wasn't on my way out. Looks like things were about to get awkward any way. Damn. I know he said that last night ain't have to be a one-time thing, but for some reason I didn't think he really meant it. People say all kinds of shit when they're trying to get off. Rather than ask him flat-out if he was serious about us hookin' up again, I thought it would be best to bounce. But I gotta admit, he looked cute in the mornin' light. The stubble along his jawline was noticeable and his hair was all crazy—half of it sticking up and the other half plastered to his head. I'm pretty sure I looked jacked and didn't even bother to find a mirror for confirmation; I could feel my eye boogers and my breath could probably start a fire, but at least I didn't have to worry about crazy hair, because I had started buzzing mine about three years ago when I noticed a widow's peak comin' in. I blame my father's shitastic genes for that. Chris smoothed his hands through his hair, making the strands all point in one direction. Much better. At least one of us was keeping up appearances.

"Yeah, why?"

"Well, I was hoping you'd at least stay and have breakfast with me. Let me order up some room service and, I don't know, talk and maybe get to know each other. We didn't exactly do too much talking last night."

"What's the point? I mean, it was just a one-night stand. I go back to my life. You go back to yours. We're good. Just gotta find my underwear and . . ."

"Aren't you quite the asshole. Here I am, extending an olive branch. I figured you had a good time and maybe we could set something up again. I was thinking with the amount of times I made you come, you'd mellow out a bit, but I guess not. You're still kind of a prick," he said before tossing the covers over his head.

His voice was muffled under the comforter, but I still heard him. "You can leave now. Would you mind closing the bedroom door on your way out? Oh, and thanks for the memories. Stay gold."

This motherfucker.

Tryna turn my words on me? Hell nah! You don't say some smartass shit and dismiss me. Who the hell did he think he was? *I'll leave when I'm ready, damnit.* I stalked over to the bed and pulled back the covers.

"You think you're funny, don't you?"

He looked up at me with a slight grin. "I do. Some might even say I'm hilarious. Figured you needed a taste of your own medicine."

Those stupid freakin' gorgeous blue eyes were gonna get me into trouble. "I want bacon."

"Yeah?" he said, smiling. "What else do you want?"

"Pancakes, too."

"Mmm, is that all?" he said, licking his lips.

"Nah, not just any pancakes—chocolate chip pancakes with warm maple syrup. It's a cheat day. I'm eating fatty shit today."

Chris leaned up and grabbed the front of my shirt, pulled me down on top of his body, and kissed me. Dude had no fear—I had morning breath that could melt the chrome off a bumper, but he ain't even care. Next thing I knew, my shirt and jeans were being tossed across the room and I was naked again. We rolled around on the bed in a tangled mess of sheets mingled with our dried cum until we landed on the floor and things got really interesting.

Room service was gonna have to wait a little bit longer.

My brain shoulda resumed its regularly scheduled program so I could jet. I had absolutely no idea what the fuck I was doing. None.

Stay With Me

I finally make it to the shower to scrub the stench of my day off my skin. The steaming hot water traveling over my stiff muscles instantly helps me unwind, and opens my mind, which ain't so relaxing. How did I let things spiral so far out of control? This situation is fucked up.

More than anything, I want to go to sleep. The buzz from the whiskey is fadin', and I wonder if I'll get the chance to finish the bottle. Surest way to put yourself into a coma-like sleep is to get drunk, and trust me, I wanna sleep like the dead. This tossing and turning while lyin' wide awake nonsense I've had the last few nights is for the birds.

Thoughts of a liquor high are interrupted by a pounding on my apartment door. *Damn, has it been an hour already?* As quickly as I can without breaking my neck, I turn off the shower, grab a towel to dry my face and hair before wrapping it around my waist, and then haul ass to my front door. The pounding does not let up.

Seriously? He's trying to make a goddamn scene? Didn't we already talk about this shit earlier?

A hoodie-covered shadow greets me through the peephole. I assume it's *him*, but in this neighborhood, you better know who you're opening your door for. I shout loud enough to be heard on the other side of the door.

"What?"

"Christ, Manny, open the door."

That voice. That soothing, bass-filled, husky voice. The voice I loved to hear whisperin' in my ear to fuck him harder just before I pulled out, ripped the condom off, and came all over his stomach.

I slip the chain off the door and undo the deadbolts. He pulls the hoodie off his head, walking past me into the apartment. I lock eyes with one of my neighbors, Mrs. Lopez in 3G, who's pushin' a bag of empty bottles in a rusty-ass shopping cart, probably headed down the block to the beer distributor near the supermarket to claim the five-cent deposit.

"You're too loud!" she yells at me as I ease the door closed.

Fuckin' witch. Her ass is makin' more noise than anyone. She's such a busybody, watchin' everything and everybody on the floor. I'm sure if I breathed wrong she'd be ready to call the cops. I try my best to respect my neighbors, especially the elderly ones, but that woman has been evil to me since I moved into the building six years ago. Some people are just mad at the world, but I got my own problems to deal with right now.

I lock the door behind Chris and then turn around; he's standing in front of my couch and starin' at me. I don't make an effort to move further into the apartment. His eyes travel up and down my water-soaked body, lingering on my towel.

His face is contorted, and for a brief moment, he looks like he's in pain. His hair stickin' up every which way— kinda gives him a boyish look. He takes a moment to smooth his hands across his hair, fully aware that the hoodie did some damage to his do. He worries his bottom lip in between his teeth, and for a second, I wanna kiss him.

I wanna shove my tongue into his mouth and feel the fire I've missed this past week, but I don't move. He jams his hands into the pockets of his dark jeans and rocks back and forth on his heels, fuckin' uncomfortable . . . and nervous. That ain't Chris. He's usually outgoing and cocky as hell.

The light I'm used to seein' in those stupid blue eyes of his ain't there. Stubble shadows his sharp jawline. He looks sad, like he wants to say something but is hesitant. God, he's fuckin' beautiful. Funny, I never thought I'd ever describe a guy as "beautiful," but that's exactly what he is. He's so perfect, and I hate his fuckin' guts for it. Hate him for makin' me fall for his ass.

"You're wet."

I look over to the iPhone dock, takin' note of the time. It's ten twenty-eight. Kinda late for Mrs. Lopez to be heading to the beer distributor by herself, but I'm sure someone'll be keepin' an eye out to see that she makes it down the block safely.

"And dripping all over the floor," he says, finishing his sentence.

I avoid eye contact and pull the towel tight around my waist, makin' sure the flap is tucked and secured.

He goes back to rocking on his heels, but instead of looking at him head-on, I focus on his sneakers: a pair of high-top black-and-white shell-toe Adidas. I know he wore 'em for my benefit. Chris knew I was an old-school sneakerhead. Gotta give him credit for tryna impress me.

"I was in the shower until you started poundin' on the door like a freakin' maniac. You want something to drink? I got juice, beer, and flavored seltzer water in the fridge. If you want somethin' harder, in the corner I've got some

Wild Turkey and Bacardi," I say, pointing to the minibar. "The Wild Turkey is pretty much done, but the rum is available."

"Thanks, I'm okay. Nothing to drink for me."

I finally meet his gaze, and he's focused on me like nothing else matters. Nothin'. No media, no celebrity status, no contracts, no being in the closet. Nothin'. He's looking at me like an apologetic lover—someone who actually cares—but I know that ain't the case. We ain't lovers. To him, we're just fuck buddies.

The unease he causes me and the way he makes me second guess myself ain't me in the least.

He unzips his hoodie and takes it off before sitting down on the couch. The thin white V-neck T-shirt clings to his broad chest, showing off all the hard work from our training sessions. He's put on at least a good twelve pounds of muscle since I began training him.

I should feel a little self-conscious about Chris being in my apartment for the first time. I mean, my apartment is a dump compared to his condo. One of his closets is probably the same square footage as my apartment, but regardless of our opposite financial statuses our differences weren't so obvious, you know? Well, at least not to me.

In the cocoon of his bedroom, he wasn't famous, he wasn't rich, he wasn't my client. There was no pretending. When I would kiss the spot on the back of his neck just below his small, crescent-moon-shaped birthmark and he'd shiver, I knew we were connected. He was mine. It was real in those moments and no one—not even Armand—could fuck with that. In my head he belonged to me.

What the fuck kind of name is Armand, anyway? That's some French elitist shit. Only parents who hate their kid would name him Armand.

"All right, I'm gonna go put some clothes on. Make yourself comfortable. The remotes for the docking station and the TV are on the coffee table," I say before heading into my bedroom.

I dry off and toss the towel onto the bed. While I search for a pair of basketball shorts in my closet, Chris walks into the room. I look down at his bare feet before my eyes travel up his body to meet his gaze. Guess he took my "make yourself comfortable" comment to heart and decided shirtless and barefoot was the way to go. The look he was givin' me, though . . . I knew that look.

With his shirt in his hand, he advanced toward me, tossing it onto the bed before pulling me in close and snakin' his arms around my neck, planting small kisses on my lips. I could feel his erection pressing against the zipper of his jeans.

"Can we make up now and get over what has you pissed?" he asked. "I've missed you, Manny. You made me wait an entire week. People on set kept asking me where you were, and I had to lie and say you were home sick with the flu."

I can't do this. I hate the way I feel. I hate Armand for makin' me face this shit. I hate that I'm jealous. I hate that I . . . I love *him*. I'm in so fuckin' deep I'm drowning. Suffocating. I can never have this man. This beautiful fucking man who makes me happy. Makes me feel good with just a smile.

I can never have him.

We can never try because of who he is. If he was just your average Joe, I could navigate this. I could try and make this shit work. I *woulda* tried because I need to know if he's my LEGO piece.

My naked daydreaming is interrupted by Chris's tongue probing my mouth. He would suck the life out of me if I let him, and I can't let him. I take a step back to break from Chris's hold, and his kiss.

He reaches for me, and I take another step back, snatching the towel off the bed to wrap around my waist, and then I lean against the closet door.

"Stay right there," I say, holding up my hands. "We need to get some shit straight."

He laughs. "God, I've missed that foul mouth of yours. It's amazing how you're the cordial professional on set, but once you let your guard down, you curse more than a sailor in a whorehouse."

It's called code-switching, but I'm not sure Chris even knows what the hell that is. I'm rough around the edges, but I'm no idiot. I know people look at me and make all kinds of assumptions, but rather than play into them, I do the complete opposite. When I'm with clients and people on set, I adapt to their language. People of color have to do this shit all the time because of racism and inequality. Yeah, sometimes we have to put on airs, because if we don't, we'll never be taken seriously. But Chris doesn't know anything about that because I've always been unfiltered and real around him. He also doesn't have to pretend to be something he's not because of his race. He may hide his sexuality, but sexual preferences ain't the shit people notice when they first meet you; skin color is.

I don't know what it is about Chris, but I've kept it real with him from day one. I've always been me. I never felt the need to be somethin' I wasn't with him. It's weird, he's way more put together than me despite being younger. To make it in Hollywood, you gotta be ready to play hardball, I guess.

Anyway, I folded my arms across my chest, making my facial expression stony as ever. He wasn't off the hook.

"Are you seriously mad about the Armand thing, Manny? He flirts with *everybody*. Both the male and female actors, the trainers, the caterers, and some of the crew, too!

He's just a natural-born flirt. You're reading too much into this."

I'd let it slip one night when we were in bed that I had aspirations of opening up my own gym. He knew I was training privately at my space in Gramercy and moonlighting at Equinox. Chris wanted to help and thought hiring me as his trainer would put more money toward my goal. He wasn't wrong. Already, I was strugglin' to pay the rent on the space, so his offer came at a pretty good time. The salary I earned my first two weeks as Chris's trainer was more than I had earned in an entire month at Equinox, so I was able to quit that job and take on training privately full-time. Most def, I was glad he believed in me enough to help me out.

One of the perks of working for your cutty buddy is that nothing was suspicious about the amount of time Chris and I spent together. His show on MFN is on hiatus for the next few months, so he took a movie role as an up-and-coming boxer. Filming started four weeks ago, and since the film was set in NYC in the early '90s, he thought it would be a great idea to hire me as his trainer. I was local, so it was convenient. We'd continue to get to know each other, and of course, fool around in his trailer when we had the time. We were six months into our arrangement and things were going pretty fuckin' well until last week.

Last week, while dickin' around with a couple of the crew and a few of the actors, Armand Robichaux, the wardrobe supervisor for the movie, decided to get a little handsy. The guy's flamboyant and non-threatening demeanor meant he got away with a lot of shit that probably would've gotten *me* arrested or sued for sexual harassment. Never liked him from day one.

In between takes, a few actors were going through lines, and of course, Armand jumped in to improvise while he casually handed out sweatshirts with the fictional gym's logo to a couple of extras who were in the next scene. First, he jokingly pretended to spar with Chris until Chris mentioned he needed to practice his lines for the scene to be shot later that afternoon with his female co-star who was also his love interest. How fuckin' upstanding of Armand to stand in as the love interest. I'm sure you could guess, for much of the scene, Chris was the object of Armand's focus. To Armand, that meant he could say all sorts of lascivious shit. Everyone was used to Armand's flirting so they all laughed it off. Chris, bein' a good sport, hammed it up for the crew, but if I ain't know better, he was more than into it. It didn't look like just acting to me, and he seemed a little reluctant to end it. That was until the applause and catcalls came from the crew of onlookers. I began to wonder if there was some shit goin' on with Armand and Chris. Suddenly, every gesture seemed too intimate and the time they spent together too much. I was second guessin' everything.

"But you flirted back. I saw you with my own eyes, and you were goading his ass on. Are you fucking him?" I asked, keeping my voice calm despite anger bubblin' under the surface.

He laughs.

I say something funny? He thinks this a joke? I am serious as a heart attack, and this motherfucker is laughing. Chris makes a move to touch me, but I step out of his reach just as his hand is about to make contact with my chest.

"You fuckin' him?" I ask again.

"Are you asking me because you're jealous, Manny, or because you're the only one who wants to be fucking me?" he says with a smirk.

What I want is to deck him. His cockiness is irritating as hell. Usually I find it hot, but not right now. Right now that shit is about as appealing as pickin' a splinter out of my finger.

I manage to ask the question again, this time raising my voice and emphasizing every word through a clenched jaw: "Are. You. Fuckin'. Him?"

Chris sighs like he's annoyed with the entire situation. "No, I'm not fucking him, and frankly, I'm pretty insulted you're asking me that," he responds with an equally raised voice.

"Why? It's not like we're exclusive or anything."

The bedroom gets so quiet, you can hear the wheels of Mrs. Lopez's cart squeaking down below through the open bedroom window. He looks at me with a mixture of shock, fear, and hate, mirroring all the feelings I had when I saw him flirting with Armand. His anguished expression makes him look as if I had punched him.

Shit. When I returned his call, I promised myself I'd control my emotions and be cool about everything but that plan is failing fast. *Get back on track, Manny. Keep it together and hold on just a little longer.*

"Look, that ain't what I meant, Chris, it's just that . . ."

He waves me off. "No. No, you're right. We're not exclusive. You can see whomever you want. If it gets physical, let me know, yeah? We're not sleeping together while you're dating someone else. Hope you understand, I have to look out for myself," he says with indifference.

I go back to folding my arms across my chest and leaning against the closet door. I wanna scream, because I know he feels this shit too—this connection or whatever—but he's too pigheaded to admit it.

"God, you're so damn stubborn! A stubborn asshole. You're so fuckin' dense, and it's frustrating," I yell, moving away from the closet door so that I'm standing face to face with Chris. *Well, so much for controlling my emotions.* I want so badly to kiss him. To kiss him and feel his body pressed against mine, but I don't move. My nostrils are flaring and my breathing is erratic, but I don't touch him.

I'm pretty sure my neighbors are wondering what the heck is going on with all the yelling. As soon as the thought crosses my mind, I hear a series of thumps on my living room wall. Mr. and Mrs. Jackson next door got some nerve knockin'. When their loud-ass grandkids come visit, you never hear me knockin' on their wall telling them to keep it the fuck down.

"So now we're turning to insults? You tell me we're not exclusive, I agree with you and say when you find someone else you'd like to date, fuck, whatever, just let me know and I'll step out of the picture, and *I'm* dense?"

"Yeah," I reply softly. My breathing starts to return to normal.

"And why am I dense, Manny?" he says, hooking his thumbs through the belt loops of his jeans, which are now hanging low, exposing his hipbones. I see a few pubes. He ain't wearing underwear. Fuck, the sight of his exposed skin is doin' a number on me.

Time to ante up. The thought of Chris being vulnerable with somebody else makes me wanna vomit. I want him to be with me, have feelings for only me.

He could fire me and tell me to go fuck myself, but this isn't just all me, I can feel it.

I hesitate. "Because, I love you. I love you, and you don't love me. And even if you did love me, we can't do shit about it. And . . . I hate . . ."

I stop talkin' and keep my attention on his feet because I realize I'm babbling.

All of the oxygen has been sucked out of the room when Chris doesn't say anything. I want him to say somethin', to acknowledge what I've laid out for him, but there's nothing. Just the sound of my heavy breathing and silence. Lots and lots of silence. I wish I was anywhere but here. I wish I had kept my mouth shut.

Just when I'm about to walk out of the room to get away from him and the awkwardness, Chris takes a step toward me. "Wait. Come again— What did you say?" he stutters.

"I love you," I repeat, lookin' down at his bare feet. I wanna get lost in those deep blue eyes of his, but I can't tear my eyes away from his feet and the floor. I feel like I just jumped off a treadmill that had been cranked up to the highest setting on the highest fuckin' incline possible. He knows. As hard as it was sayin' the words, I'm glad I did. I feel . . . relieved.

I was just happy that I had to the balls to say somethin', but while I'm ready to celebrate that victory, Chris catches me off guard with a little confession of his own. "I—I love you, too," he stammers.

I force my gaze up. He's staring at me with such . . . I dunno, kindness? Adoration? Understanding? He's never looked at me like that before, and it's making my insides feel all kinds of fucked up—fucked up in a good way, though.

The layers of bullshit are gone and it's finally just us, the real us. The us who talk into the wee hours of the morning while I stroke his back and he runs a hand down my chest. The us who aren't always on guard.

"I think I knew I'd probably fall for you the morning after we had sex for the first time and you told me you wanted pancakes and bacon. Who says that? Not just any pancakes, though, they had to be chocolate chip pancakes with warm maple syrup. You were just as demanding then as you are now."

I smile at his comment. Shit, I was hungry.

"All I kept thinking was, wouldn't it be something if I ended up with this guy. So blunt, so strong-willed, so attractive.

"You're everything I'm not, Manny. You're the complete opposite of me, and I think that's why this thing is good. I think that's why our connection works, and I think that's why I'm crazy about you. I've wanted to say that for a long time, but I didn't think you wanted to hear it. I didn't think you wanted something more."

I sit down on the bed but Chris doesn't make a move to join me. He's crazy about me. All this time I was thinkin' this was one-sided. I was losin' sleep over this shit and he was crazy about me. Life is a surprise every damn day. So unpredictable.

"Looks like our arrangement with you being my trainer worked out even better than we could've imagined. It's the perfect way for us to be together."

I'm still processing that he loves me back. This shit is warm and comforting, but I'm also feeling uneasy. Nauseous even. I should be geeked. I should be bouncin' off the damn walls with happiness, but my gut tells me somethin' ain't right.

For the moment, at least, I'm trying to let these feelings of uneasiness go. Whatever it is, I'm sure it'll pass, but I'm skeptical that way. I'll let it go for now because I'm just happy to have him in my apartment, even though it's dangerous for him to be here.

He walks over to me and straddles my lap, and then hooks his arms around my neck to pull me in for a kiss. My dick is happy with the outcome. This went over better than I ever coulda imagined. I had no reason to be scared over some bullshit. Chris isn't with Armand, and he loves me back.

Now we could try and figure out what to do next. I'd have to find some way to break it to Juan that I was not only bisexual but also seeing the *loco* he watched on MFN every Sunday. And breakin' that news to Pablo and mi abuela Rosa, fuck. That was gonna be an interesting discussion to tackle, but I'd worry about it later. Right now I have a partially naked man straddlin' my dick.

Once I get Chris outta his jeans we can move on with making up.

Frantically, I reach for his zipper as he gently bites my lower lip.

"Gotta get you outta these pants," I say, pulling my lips from his. I reverse our positions and push him down on his back, making moves to get those damn jeans off. Finally, his dick is free, and he's just as excited as I am. I missed him. I missed us being together like this.

"Where's the lube and condoms?" he asks.

I stretch over Chris's body to dig into my nightstand drawer. Once I have a condom and lube in hand, I crush my mouth against his, lovin' the familiar taste of him. And his smell . . . so distinct but kinda indescribable. It's crazy how much the man lying beneath me had become a part of me. One thing's for sure: I missed his uncut cock. I haven't had sex since I stopped returning his calls, and I've been so damn *bellaco*. I'm probably hornier than a bitch in heat. I can't wait to peel his foreskin back and get that fat cockhead in my mouth.

I break our embrace and sit up, leaning back on my heels. I start strokin' my dick, and Chris touches himself while watchin' me.

Watching his foreskin glide back and forth over the head of his dick is such a fuckin' turn on. His cock is perfect. I know everyone ain't into the extra skin, but that shit is so hot to me. Chris follows my lead and sits up so we're both kneeling on the bed and facing each other. He grabs the bottle of lube and pours a few drops onto his dick. I keep strokin' myself while watching him oil up. He is sportin' some wood, not fully hard but gettin' close.

Chris plants kisses along the crook of my neck and jawline before returning to my lips. He doesn't miss a beat. It's like we were never apart. He delivers a trail of kisses down my chest and stops at my nipples. His tongue swirls around a nipple, which made my dick even harder. Shit. Everything about this feels good. I missed his mouth. I missed his tongue. But out of all the things I missed most about Chris, not feeling his touch took the biggest toll.

And as if knowing what I'm thinking, Chris grabs my dick and pumps his hand up and down. God, his hand feels incredible, all slick from the lube so the glide is extra smooth. I grab hold of his dick to give him the same amount of attention, but he gently pushes my hand away.

"No. Let me do this," he says, nipping at my lips.

Who am I to say no?

Chris rubs our dicks together, and the sensation is so intense. His grip on my dick is rough but gentle. Real fuckin' nice. I fondle his dick, rubbing the buildup of precum with my thumb back and forth over the head of his cock, pushing his foreskin back. The lube is a satisfying addition; it makes my movements sleek. Chris lets go of my dick, touching the tip of his cock to mine, using both hands to stretch his foreskin, and then pulls the skin over the head of my cock. When the skin is stretched to its limit, he holds it in place with his thumb and proceeds to jerk us both off. I moan into his mouth while his slicked-up hand works its magic. Fuck, it feels so good.

I thrust my hips forward, causing little jolts of electricity to course through my balls. I'm in heaven. Between Chris's pace and his little whimpers and grunts, I'm gonna lose it real soon. *Real* soon.

"Wait, shit, slow down or I'm gonna come before we even get to fuck," I pant out between strokes.

"Mmm, but this is your favorite," he says, his tongue trailing over my lips.

Fuck. This is *so* my favorite. I love docking. We'd only recently starting doin' it before shit went south. Chris hadn't ever done it and had been kinda self-conscious about it. I have no idea why—his dick is fuckin' perfection to me. He also hadn't had many sexual partners to share his kinks with; maybe he wasn't used to someone being so open about what they liked.

Once we'd fucked more than a handful of times, I knew this was something I was gonna eventually do with him. I had to feel secure enough to talk about what I liked, you know? Writin' it on a profile was one thing, actually talkin' about fetishes and kinks with someone you're fuckin' was another. Initially, he had been kinda shy when he wanted sex rougher than normal or for me to whisper dirty shit in his ear while I tagged that pretty ass of his doggy style.

We had developed a comfortable sexual relationship that turned into many late nights of fuckin' and talkin' until we passed out. I loved and hated those nights. Hated them because it was hell for me, because I got up at five a.m. every day, but it was worth it because I knew it was the only private time we'd have together. I came to enjoy those late nights way more than I let on, but I don't have to worry about sneaking around anymore because Chris cares. He cares about me like I care about him. We . . . we love each other. I can't believe this is actually happening. I'm finally getting the sweaty-palms, heart-palpitation shit, and it feels . . . good. It feels real. The dude who was so fuckin' unlucky in love ends up fallin' for a hookup. Crazy shit for real.

My hand covers Chris's and I speed up his pace as he jerks our cocks together and I come. "Jesus . . . fuck!" I growl when my orgasm hits. I come so fuckin' hard I feel like I'm about to black out.

A week's worth of frustration went into that orgasm, and I'm spent. I'm basically a useless sack of bones. Chris reaches his climax right behind me. He lets out a groan, and when he pulls back his foreskin, thick droplets of cum drizzle onto the bedspread. Yeah, we made a fuckin' mess. Chris gives me a soft kiss on the lips, continuing a trail of kisses down my chest before his warm mouth closes over my cock. He licks and swallows up every last bit of cum on my dick. I look down at his head bobbin' while he takes me whole. My dick is softening, but that doesn't stop Chris. He's concentratin' pretty hard down there, but I'm feeling both wired and tired.

Chris's tongue circles around the head of my dick as he creates a suction like he's trying to drain me dry. I softly push his head back—dude is gonna fuckin' end me if he keeps this up.

"Easy, easy, sensitive," I murmur.

"Sorry," he says, looking up at me with a half-hearted smile.

He jerks back, but not before givin' my dick one long lick up and down the shaft. That mouth of his is pretty fuckin' special.

His erection begins to soften, and I think it's only fair to clean off whatever cum hasn't landed on the bedspread. I lean down between his thighs and take his cock into my mouth, makin' sure I'm just as thorough as he was. My tongue traces a path over his foreskin before pushing it back. I suck gently and squeeze Chris's balls, delivering a small amount of pressure. Before shit went off the rails, I discovered that he liked a little cock-and-ball torture.

The harder I squeeze his nuts, the louder he moans.

"You know what makes you so hot?" I say, collapsing beside him, making sure to move up a bit so we can avoid the cum circle on the bedspread.

"You mean aside from my good looks and charm?"

"Yeah, other than that," I reply, folding my arms behind my head.

"No. Why don't you tell me?" he says, inching closer to me and tossing a leg over mine.

"You love me. That makes you hot."

"Hotter, you mean."

"Yeah, hotter, whateva," I responded, laughin'. "Gimme like fifteen minutes and I'll be ready to fuck. I just gotta catch my breath. Damn, that was good."

Chris tilts his head up against my shoulder and smiles, his fingers circling my stomach. "Okay, you'd better rest up then. The timer starts now."

I take my hand from behind my head and move it up and down his spine as he leans into me. This time I can touch him—really touch him—without him thinkin' I'm being clingy. Now that everything is out in the open, I'm looking forward to touching him as much as I want.

"You know, I gotta figure out what I'm gonna tell Juan. If I'm gonna be in a relationship with a man, he needs to know. My moms won't be a problem, but Juan, yeah. I gotta have the conversation about me being bi first before I drop the bomb about me being with a dude he regularly watches on TV."

Chris turns to me and looks panicked. "You can't tell him, Manny," he blurts out.

My eyes narrow. I'm not liking where this is going. I stop stroking his back and sit up on the bed. "What do you mean I can't tell him?"

I don't wanna make assumptions, but is he ashamed of me or some shit? I know I'm not prissy or rich, but I ain't think any of that mattered to Chris. I'm starting to wonder if I'm what he really wants. Did he say he loves me only because I said it first?

"You can't tell Juan. You can't tell your mother. You can't tell your aunt. You can't tell anyone. If we're going to be together, it has to be in secret. No one can know we're seeing each other."

And there it is.

I shoulda known shit was too good to be true. This is always the case. Anytime somethin' seems like smooth sailing, it ends up a disaster. I swear it's the story of my motherfuckin' life.

"Hold up. I tell you I love you. You tell me you love me. We beat off together, and now you're tellin' me I gotta go on keepin' this shit between us a secret?"

"Yes, Manny, that's what I'm saying," he replies, running his fingers through what's left of his hair. It was cut low with the sides and back slightly shorter than the top for the movie, which worked out great, since Chris would've had to cut his hair anyway for an upcoming story arc on *Blue Law*. Turns out, Chris's character was going to be working undercover with the New Jersey State Police to infiltrate a neo-Nazi chapter in Hunterdon County. I was startin' to get used to the close-cropped look on him, although I preferred him with longer hair.

"You can't tell anyone about us. Now isn't the time for me to come out. My career is picking up. I'm hot right now, Manny. The ratings for *Blue Law* are through the roof and there's talk of an Emmy nomination. More movie roles are being pitched to my agent. Things are really kicking off for me. I can't mess that up by coming out *and* telling the world that I have a boyfriend I've been secretly seeing."

It takes me a few minutes to process everything he just said. I lift off the bed—I can't be next to him. I can't believe he twisted his mouth to say that nonsense. He acts like instead of me just confessing my feelings, I asked him for the weather. I went out on a fuckin' limb because I couldn't take hidin' my feelings, but he don't even blink twice before tellin' me to keep pretendin'. Chris just became a grade-A asshole for that.

"So this means there is no 'us' then. Is that what you're saying?" I'm struggling to keep the edge out of my voice, but I know I'm failing horribly. Ain't no way to hide being pissed. But I'm not just pissed, I'm hurt. Chris has made this all about him. Like he's the only one who would be risking shit by coming out. Like I wouldn't have to deal with scrutiny from family, some friends, and maybe even some colleagues, too. Some of my friends know about me, but most of them don't. Seems like Chris has never once thought about how him being with me would impact my life. He ain't the only one sacrificing. I knew what I was dealing with and what would likely come once word got out.

"No, Manny. That's not what I'm saying. There's still an 'us', but no one can know about it. We can't be out publicly. I have to think about what's best for my career, and right now, I don't think coming out is a wise choice."

"Nah. Hell nah. I tell you I'm ready to out myself to everybody to be with your ass. I'm ready to tell my family, my friends, and you fix your mouth to say you can't because you don't wanna mess up your career? You selfish motherfucker.

"About twenty minutes ago you told me you loved me, and you knew you were fallin' for me a long time ago, now you say this shit? Nah. That ain't cool."

I grab my towel off the edge of the bed and wrap it around my waist before chancing a glance at Chris.

His face is unreadable. "What are you saying, Manny?"

I have never been the ultimatum type. Someone tells me I gotta do something *or else* is the quickest way for me to not give a shit. I don't like being pressured, so I'd never ask that of another person, but right now . . . right now I'm leading the ultimatum campaign.

He can't have his cake and eat it too. He can't tell me he feels a certain type of way about me but then have an escape clause attached. Either he's with me or he ain't. We're in it together or there ain't no "us." Chris will either realize he's being a dick and change his mind or . . . or . . . He wouldn't just give this up, would he?

"I'm sayin' either we're doing this and you wanna give it a shot or we're done. I'm not gonna be a dirty little secret. We're gonna start this off right, or we ain't doin' it at all, Chris. I already have a fucked-up track record when it comes to relationships, and starting on a bad note with you just seems like awful fuckin' karma. I don't wanna do that.

"I wanna have a fair shot. I wanna make this work. I *need* to make this work, but starting out with lies ain't the way."

Before the words even come out of his mouth, I can tell he's ready to let me go. I'm glad I mean that little to him, that he can make a decision on the fly and that's it. Like the last six months ain't even happen, like those three little words ain't come out of his mouth twenty minutes ago.

Love ain't all it's cracked up to be. For the first time, I realize that love is one cruel-ass joke. It makes you believe that anything is possible.

Love is a goddamn lie.

The only people who will ever love me are Moms, Juan, and Titi Lucia. They're the only people I can count on. They're the only people who'll have my back and never do me wrong.

"Manny, I can't risk a relationship right now. You have to recognize why. It's not that I don't love you. I do. God, I swear I do, it's just . . . it's just not the right time for us to go public."

"Then I guess we have our answer. This is over and done. Get your shit and get out."

Pissed and betrayed, I don't ever want to see this motherfucker again. I'm stupid for thinking this would be different. The one time I let myself fall for someone and actually see if it could really work, I get told I ain't worth the risk. Fine, Chris cares more about his career, that's cool. I made the mistake of letting this go on for too damn long anyway. I deserve this.

"Manny? Are you sure about this?"

"What part of 'get your shit and get out' don't you understand? You made your choice, Christopher. Lose my number, and by the way, I quit. Find yourself another trainer."

If I'm going out, I'm doin' it in a blaze of glory.

I sit on the edge of the bed and keep my back to him the entire time he gets dressed. He doesn't say another word, which is good because I'm done talking anyway.

I don't move until I hear the front door close shut.

My eyes well up and a couple of unexpected tears roll down my cheeks, and then I break down. The last time I cried like this was when Moms told me my pops wasn't comin' back. I remember that like it was yesterday. Feelin' like I wasn't good enough. Like something I did made him leave. Like, if my own father didn't love me enough to stay, no one else would either.

Dark Times

To say the next couple of months were rough is putting it mad nice. I busied myself with work to forget about everything. Mainly, I did it to forget about the biggest mistake of my life. Even without Chris's help, I had built up enough of a client base where I was doing okay and actually gaining momentum in the personal training field.

My schedule was booked, and I was looking at spaces to make the final stages of my dream into reality. The realtor I'd been working with, Dawn, was pretty chill— well, not at first. It took a while for me and Dawn to find a groove. The look she gave me when I stepped into her office pretty much told me she ain't think I was good enough to earn her business, but money talks. After being a complete *bicha* for the better part of an hour, she realized I was the real deal. Most people woulda left and taken their business elsewhere, but wherever I went, there would be another Dawn. There would always be someone questioning my intentions, qualifications, and credit history.

Don't let my appearance fool you. I can only assume she thought I was some sort of gangbanger or drug dealer, because you know, that's all Latinos are good for, right? Imagine us being entrepreneurs. Stereotypes are a motherfucker. Dawn, and people like her, is exactly why I wanted my own shit. When you're the boss, can't nobody turn their nose up at you. Funny how perspective changes when money enters the equation.

We had to work through some rough patches. She kept showing me spaces on the Upper East Side, which wasn't at all what I was goin' for. I wasn't tryna teach yoga classes to trust-fund brats and socialites. I was tryna attract clients who were more into bodybuilding.

Just when I was about to put in an offer on a space on Sixth Ave, she showed me a warehouse loft space that opened up not too far from Fulton Street near the South Street Seaport. It was the perfect spot for my new and improved gym studio: close enough to mass transit and in an area that was likely to attract high-end clients from all walks of life.

It'd been three months since Chris and I parted ways. I'd buried myself in work . . . and sex. I was hookin' up a couple times a week with men and women. Even went on a couple dates and tried to really give 'em a fair shot. I don't discriminate, although this last month, I'd been seeing a lot more men. I'd been scarce with my family and not coming around as much, missing out on chillin' with Juan, until finally, when I was at my mom's place grabbin' Sunday dinner, everybody decided it was time for an intervention.

"Manny, what's been going on with you, mi amor?" my mother asks while fixing me a plate of *pernil y arroz con gandules y platanos*. Moms would never cook a meal this big except for Christmas, but she knows the best way to get me to visit is to cook some bangin' food.

Juan is sitting at the kitchen table with his girlfriend, Marisol, on his lap while they play Candy Crush on his phone. Titi Lucia is lookin' up at me expectantly but with a frown on her face.

"Answer your mother, Emmanuel," my titi says with a voice that makes me feel like a kid again, but I'm a grown-ass man gettin' chewed out. I know shit is serious because she called me Emmanuel. She never calls me that. Ever.

"We haven't seen you for months. When you finally do come around, you're brooding and have an attitude. Why aren't you happy? You just opened a new business."

"In an expensive-ass neighborhood, too. *Chacho*, how'd you swing that?" Juan chimes in. "You robbin' banks on the side, bro?" he says with a laugh.

I take a seat next to Titi Lucia and Moms sets the plate of food down in front me. I really wanna eat since everything smells and looks so good, but everyone is staring at me, even Marisol.

"What?" I say, a bit more defensive than I intend.

My mother tilts my chin up to meet her eyes. *"¿Cual es el problema, mi amor?"* Of course she's gonna ask me what's wrong. Moms can always tell when shit ain't right.

I sigh. This ain't how I wanted to tell my family, but they need to know. God, I hope Juan can handle this. I don't want shit to change between us.

Gently, I tug my chin outta my mother's grasp, stab a piece of roast pork, and pop it into my mouth. At least I could get a taste of the food before my appetite decides to abandon me once I get all this shit out in the open. I swallow hard before I start talking.

"A couple of months ago, I started seeing someone."

My mother's face lights up when I look at her.

"That's cool, bro," Juan replies. "When do we get to meet her?"

I wince. Moms notices the change in my body language, and I know she knows before I even say a word.

"You don't. It's over anyway."

"What? What happened?" Juan asks.

I look over at Titi Lucia, and it's as if her and Moms are communicatin' telepathically. She knows too.

Might as well treat this shit like a Band-Aid and let the news come hard and fast before I change my mind. I only hope that Juan still treats me the same after all is said and done. I didn't want him to find out this way, but since everyone's askin', I'd rather say it once and be done.

I look over at Juan, and he's beaming, bouncing Marisol on his lap. She's taken over the game and has pretty much tuned us all out. They make a cute couple. I hope Juan marries her. They've been livin' together for a year and a half but have been dating since high school. I kinda hope Marisol is it for him—she's a nice girl and from a good family. A good fit for Juan, since she keeps him honest and on top of his game.

"Ain't no easy way to say this, so I'm just gonna say it. You can ask me whatever you want after. Cool?"

Marisol looks up from the phone, and Juan shifts her on his lap, asking, "What's up, Emmanuel?"

I take a deep breath and let 'er rip.

"I wasn't seeing a girl, a woman. I was um . . . dating a guy. His name is Chris. I'm bisexual, and we were involved for a bit before things got too serious and I . . . we . . . called it off."

Both Marisol and Juan stare at me, stunned. Juan's mouth is parted in an O, but he quickly closes it.

He scratches the back of his head with this goofy-ass look on his face, and Marisol looks down at the tablecloth, her cheeks flushing. Moms and Titi Lucia are quiet.

"Now's the time to speak up if you got some shit to say, Juan. Let it out."

Moms frowns at me. She hates when I curse.

"I-I had no idea you were gay, um, bi."

"Not something I go around shouting since who I fu . . . uh, have sex with is nobody's business."

"Moms, you and Titi Lucia are quiet. Too quiet. You knew?" he asks.

Moms nods at Juan. *"Sí."*

My mother grabs my brother's hand and gives it a little squeeze. "Juan, I love you both no matter what. Manny is an adult and he's living his life. He knows I care about him protecting himself and being safe more than anything. Doesn't matter if he's with a woman or a man. *A mí no me corresponde, ni es mi derecho, juzgar a alguien a base de su orientación sexual."*

Moms is saying that judging me, or anybody, on the grounds of their sexual orientation isn't her business nor her right. I've never loved my mother more than I do in this moment. She let everyone in the room know that her job was to love me, and never judge. Moms displayed exactly what unconditional love is.

Titi Lucia chimes in, "He's your brother. Nothing about him has changed. He's the same guy you grew up with. The one who made you breakfast, helped you with your homework when your mother was working, washed your pissy sheets when you wet the bed, taught you how to fight and how to shoot a basketball. He was the father you should've had if yours wasn't a deadbeat loser. Manny loves you no matter what, and you'd better feel the same, Juan." Titi Lucia's voice is threatening as she wags a finger at my brother.

"Okay, okay, let's chill out and let Juan process this for a sec. We cool or what?" I ask, staring at him. Marisol lifts off his lap and excuses herself. Titi Lucia follows her and Moms takes a seat at the table.

Juan ain't looking at me. He's shifting in his chair, kinda nervous-like. "I guess. Ain't my business. It's just a little weird to think of you with a guy, but okay, whatever. We're cool," he says, finally meeting my gaze.

I stretch out my hand, and he gives me a pound.

Moms clasps her hands over ours and smiles. "My boys. You both make me proud."

Now that that awkwardness is over with, I turn my attention back to my plate—my food is getting cold. I shove a plantain in my mouth and start chewing.

"So what happened with you and the Chris guy?" Juan asks.

I start a coughing fit. Moms pats me on the back before heading to the sink and returning with a glass of water. She hands it to me just as my coughing dies down a little.

Now he has questions . . . shoulda known better.

"Thanks," I say once I catch my breath. "Uh . . ." I push the rice around the plate before taking a couple of bites. "You know that show on MFN? *Blue Law*?"

"Hell yeah! That's my shit," Juan yells excitedly.

Moms swats him on the back of his head. "Language. You and Manny with your cursing. Watch your mouth."

"Sorry," we both say at the same time. She knows it's almost impossible for us to watch our mouths when we're hyped about something.

"So what about *Blue Law*? What's that got to do with who you were dating?"

As soon as the words come out of his mouth it's like a lightbulb goes off.

"No way! You were dating somebody on the show?"

"Uh . . . I was dating the star of the show."

"No fuckin' way!"

Moms delivers two hard slaps to the back of Juan's head. *"Cuida tu lenguaje. Asi no fué como yo te crié."* She raised us better than this? Pssh. Our cursing has nothing to do with how she raised us. Moms knows how shit goes down when Juan and I get together.

"Ma! He was dating Christopher Kaine. Christopher Kaine! That's a big deal. He's like one of the top up-and-coming actors in Hollywood. That guy is everywhere now."

"That doesn't excuse your language, Juan."

"Fine. Fine, sorry! But Ma, check it, this is big."

He yells toward the living room, "Marisol, Titi Lucia, come here, you gotta hear this."

I groan when my aunt and Marisol come back into the kitchen.

"The guy that Manny's been giving hot sausage injections to is Chris Kaine. Dude on that show *Blue Law* on MFN!"

Both Marisol and Titi Lucia stare at me in disbelief. Moms is unmoved. She don't watch much television except for her telenovelas.

"Wh-what happened between you two?" Juan asks.

"He was cool with being in the closet, I wasn't, so it's done. I really don't wanna talk about it anymore. All I ask is that you don't ask me about it no more, and don't tell nobody."

"You can trust us," Juan says.

Moms pulls me close to her hip and gives me a hug. As soon as she wraps her arms around me, I bury my face in her apron and bite my lip to choke back a sob. Ain't no way I'm gonna lose it in front of my family.

Chris is behind me. I need to move on.

———

"Just one more set. You can do this. You got this, Matt. And five-four-three-two-one."

"Fuck!" Matt shouts.

The bar clangs when Matt sets it back on the rack.

"It's all over now. Take a breather for a minute and then give me a couple sets of plate pushes. I want four sets of ten."

"Damn, Manny. Can I rest longer than a minute? Can I get at least five?"

"Nope. You get a minute, and it starts now."

I walk toward the back of the studio while Matt sits up from the flat weight bench, breathing heavily. He's my first client of the day, and I'm feeling good this particular morning—until I decided to head to the water fountain and grab a drink. The TV mounted to the wall has the volume turned down low, but not low enough. Something about *Blue Law* catches my attention, so I turn up the volume and read the news ticker scrolling across the bottom of the screen.

Christopher Kaine has just been nominated for his first Emmy: Outstanding Lead Actor in a Drama Series for his portrayal of Police Detective Michael O'Rourke on the MFN original series Blue Law.

Like I said, I was feeling great . . . until that announcement.

After I finish training my client, I have my receptionist, Sarah, cancel the rest of my appointments. I am in no condition to be around people. I'd likely injure someone by not paying attention. I don't need a lawsuit, so it's best to shut the operation down for the rest of the day.

I guess Chris's sacrifice was worth it. He was making a name for himself in Hollywood. Everything worked out fuckin' perfectly for him. He's just been nominated for an Emmy.

Now I guess I can get what I want: to lose myself in the moment and forget about everything from the day. Fuck the Emmys. Fuck Christopher. Fuck it all.

I follow the cute twink into the bathroom stall, and he drops to his knees, clawing at my zipper before I can even shut the door. He'd been eyein' me since I stepped foot in the bar. It's like he could sense I needed to release some tension, and I intend to release all right. Release and forget about this fuckin' empty feeling I've had for the last few months.

I drown out everything and instead concentrate on the sweet mouth that's lickin' my balls.

———

I have over 800 cable channels, yet I'm sitting here watching the Emmys. I ain't completely pathetic, though, I just tuned in for the last hour. That's normally when they present the big awards in the Best Actor and Best Actress categories, I think.

What the fuck is wrong with me? I'm never gonna get over Chris if I keep up with what's going on with him, but I'm secretly hoping he wins. If he was willing to ditch a relationship with me, I wanted him to at least do well. Maybe this'll make it all worthwhile. I doubt it, but I guess I need to know that there is some kind of payoff for the empty fuckin' feeling that won't go away.

I go grab my food and a beer from the kitchen and start chowing down at the right time because Chris's category is up.

The cameras focus on all the nominees, anticipating their reactions when the winner is announced.

"And the award for Outstanding Lead Actor in a Drama Series goes to . . . Christopher Kaine for his role as Detective Michael O'Rourke in Blue Law.*"*

Applause bursts from the audience and music plays.

Wow, he won. He fuckin' won! *¡Wepa!* I can't help but be a little proud of him.

Chris stands at his seat and freezes as the camera zooms in on his face, and his mouth falls open. The camera pans out and I see his sister, Aimee, reach for him, wrapping her arms around his neck and pulling him close. Her face is hidden behind Chris's head, but he nods and then kisses her on the cheek before he adjusts his jacket and squares his shoulders as if he's entering a boxing ring. He looks so . . . so . . . different. His demeanor is both relaxed and defiant, as if to say, "I had this shit in the bag." His eyes look determined and his jaw is set hard. This is not the Chris I was used to seeing. This is a more confident Chris. It kinda makes me sad to see the change, but I can't lie, I'm intrigued by this new version of the man. He needed to take control of his career and I'm happy for him in that regard, but starin' at him for too long is too painful.

Memories of what coulda been start to play out in my head, and that shit ain't good for my health, so I focus on Aimee instead. She looks way better than the pictures I've seen around Chris's apartment. Her round blue eyes are the first thing I notice. They're bright as fuck, just like Chris's. After a few handshakes and slaps on the back, Chris exits the row and makes his way to the stage.

He accepts his award from the guy who plays Don Draper on *Mad Men*, giving him a quick bro hug before stepping to the microphone. The music fades, and Chris pauses for a moment to remove a blue-and-white piece of paper from his inside left breast pocket.

I'm staring at my TV so hard—I don't want to miss a minute of his win. I'm so angry with him but so fuckin' proud.

He's beautiful up there, and damn, can he wear a tux. The camera zooms in so I can see his blue eyes shimmer—he has every right to be proud of himself. He's worked so fuckin' hard and gave up so much. . . .

I shift in my seat, my throat tightening. I know what he gave up for his career. Me.

Stupid emotions. Moms' leftovers ain't appealing no more, so I set my plate on the coffee table and lean forward, resting my elbows on my knees, my hands on my head, wishing there was some hair there to tug.

This beautiful pain in my ass has had a mainline to my emotions from jump. I should hate him for it, but I can't.

Chris clears his throat. *"Thank you to the Academy for this huge honor. Working on* Blue Law *has been a dream come true. For four amazing years, I've worked on a show with such an impeccable cast of amazing talent. Our writers are spectacular, and I never know what to expect. Each time I read a script, I'm never really sure what's going to happen with my character. Leanne, Taylor, and Ed have put him through the wringer. Their writing skills are phenomenal.*

"Michael has been to hell and back but still manages to grow and forge ahead, making his place in the world. Playing a character with so much depth and emotional vulnerability has taught me a lot. Thank you to MFN for taking a chance on an unknown actor."

There's a shout from the audience telling Chris to "do it." Award shows are weird, and celebrities use it for personal platforms all the time, from Brando to DiCaprio. Chris never was very vocal about any particular issue except working hard for his family, but considering the state of our relationship, there's obviously a lot I don't know about the guy.

He narrows his eyes but there's a smile on his lips. *"My kid sister, Aimee, ladies and gents."*

There's light laughter from the audience and the camera cuts to Chris's sister sitting next to his empty seat, all red-faced but proud.

"I've never been one to talk much about my personal life, but right now you all are about to get a rare peek. I just won an Emmy, but the one other person I wanted with me tonight isn't here, and that's my fault. I put my career before love. He deserved better than

what I was willing to give. While I'm thankful for the acknowledgment of my work, it doesn't have as much meaning since he's not here to share this moment with me."

Chris unfolds the paper he took out of his jacket pocket and holds it up to the audience. Then he looks directly into the camera like he's talkin' to me only. I can't believe he's such a sap.

He kept that Blue Moon label all this time. . . . *"Parabicho,"* I mumble under my breath. He's always been a sappy cocktease.

"Emmanuel, I love you, baby." Chris holds up his Emmy. *"But this award just doesn't mean as much without you by my side."*

He takes a small bow.

"Thank you all and good night!"

The orchestra plays music into a commercial break, and I'm sittin' on my couch a shocked and teary fuckin' mess.

The End... Or is it?

Author's Note

Thank you for purchasing this novella and continuing to follow the characters of The Kinky Connect Chronicles! I appreciate your support. If you have a moment, please consider leaving a review on your preferred platform.
Reviews help authors hone their craft.
All feedback is welcomed.
Reviews also help prospective readers choose a story that may be worth their time and money. Thank you again for taking a chance on me and my work.
Want to find out what happens next in Manny and Chris's tale? Visit the Members Only area of kinkysinglesconnect.com and enter access code **UY8W9**. The passcode is case-sensitive, please use all caps. You'll find the remainder of the story there. Users of older digital devices and some smartphones may encounter difficulty connecting to the website. In that case, content is best viewed on a desktop or laptop computer.
Technology. *sigh*

STAY CONNECTED:
www.authorharpermiller.com

Sign up for exclusive content, ARC opportunities, and giveaways by joining my newsletter.

About the Author

Harper Miller is a thirty-something native New Yorker. She's traveled the world and lived in a variety of places but always finds her way back to the Big Apple. A lackluster love life leaves time to explore new interests; for Harper it is writing. *The Sweetest Taboo: An Unconventional Romance* is her debut novel. In her mind, the perfect Alpha male possesses intellect, humor, and a kinky streak that rivals the size of California.

When she isn't writing, Harper utilizes her graduate degree in the field of medical research. She enjoys fitness-related activities, drinking copious amounts of wine, and going on bad dates.

GLOSSARY OF TERMS FEATURED IN COMPLEXITY

Bicho quejón — whiny bitch

Yo podría quejarme — I might complain

Cacos — thugs/burglars/low-lifes

Asopao — A type of Puerto Rican rice soup that can be made with chicken, pork, beef, or shrimp. It's a cross between soup and paella.

Pasteles — Puerto Rican version of a tamale. Popular in Puerto Rico and many Latin American countries.

Sopa de salchichón — Puerto Rican sausage soup. Usually eaten as a comfort food.

Pendejo — dumbass, slow-witted, idiot, asshole

Loco — Usually translated as "crazy" but can also be used to address someone as "dude."

Mierda — shit

Boricua — A synonym for Puerto Rican.

Papi — hot guy

Corillos — friends, homies, crew

Chotas — snitches, tattletales

Bugarróns — derogatory term for homosexuals

Coño — fuck, damnit

Come mierda — stuck up/arrogant shit

Bellaco — horny

Bicha — bitch

Pernil y arroz con gandules — Puerto Rican meal of roast pork shoulder and rice with pigeon peas.

platanos — plaintains

Chacho — In the context of the story "Daaaammmmn" (as in to place emphasis on something). Example: Chacho! Last night I got so wasted.

Wepa — That's great! Congrats! Such great news! An expression of glee.

Parabicho — cocktease